Raising Faith

Boarding School Mysteries

Vanished (Book One)
Betrayed (Book Two)
Burned (Book Three)
Poisoned (Book Four)

Sophie's World

Sophie's World
Sophie's Secret
Sophie Under Pressure
Sophie Steps Up
Sophie's First Dance
Sophie's Stormy Summer
Sophie's Friendship Fiasco
Sophie and the New Girl
Sophie Flakes Out
Sophie Loves Jimmy
Sophie's Drama
Sophie Gets Real

The Girls of Harbor View

Girl Power (Book One)
Take Charge (Book Two)
Raising Faith (Book Three)
Secret Admirer (Book Four)

The Lucy Series

Lucy Doesn't Wear Pink (Book One)
Lucy Out of Bounds (Book Two)
Lucy's Perfect Summer (Book Three)
Lucy Finds Her Way (Book Four)

Check out www.faithgirlz.com

faiThGirLz!

GIRLS OF HARBOR VIEW

Raising Faith

Melody Carlson

ZONDERkidz™

ZONDERVAN.com/
AUTHORTRACKER
follow your favorite authors

ZONDERKIDZ

Raising Faith
Copyright © 2008, 2012 by Melody Carlson

Run Away
Copyright © 2008, 2012 by Melody Carlson

This title is also available as a Zondervan ebook.
Visit www.zondervan.com/ebooks.

Requests for information should be addressed to:
Zondervan, 5300 Patterson Ave. SE, Grand Rapids, Michigan 49530

ISBN: 978-0-310-73047-7

Editor: Kim Childress
Cover design: Cindy Davis

Printed in the United States of America

12 13 14 15 16 17 18 19 20 /DCI/ 19 18 17 16 15 14 13 12 11 10 9 8 7 6 5 4 3 2 1

So we fix our eyes not on what is seen, but on what is unseen, since what is seen is temporary, but what is unseen is eternal.

— 2 Corinthians 4:18

chapter one

"A ski trip!" Morgan controlled herself from jumping up and down in the church parking lot. "This is gonna be totally awesome, Emily."

Emily frowned. "Yeah, for some kids."

"What do you mean?"

"I mean I can't afford to go."

"But Cory said there would be ways to earn money."

Emily just shook her head. "I don't think he meant the cost for the whole trip, Morgan. Besides we're supposed to put down a fifty dollar deposit. There's no way I can do that."

"Where's your faith, Emily?"

"Not in my pocketbook, that's for sure."

"You know what I mean. Why can't you just trust God to provide?" asked Morgan.

"I try to trust him to provide for most things … but a ski trip? Well, that might be pushing it."

"You think it's too big for God?" Morgan twisted a beaded braid between her fingers as she studied her best friend's expression.

"Well, maybe not too big for God … maybe it's just too big for me," said Emily.

"Come on," urged Morgan, "don't give up just like that. You can at least ask God whether or not he wants you to go, Emily."

Emily nodded. "Yeah, I guess you're right."

"If it makes you feel any better, I don't have enough money to go either."

"Enough money for what?" asked Mom as she and Grandma joined the girls by the car.

"The youth group is taking a ski trip, including snowboarding and skiing," said Morgan.

"When is that?" asked Grandma.

"It's more than a month away," explained Morgan. "Not until after Christmas."

"How much?" asked Mom as she unlocked the car.

"Two hundred dollars!" exclaimed Emily.

"Goodness," said Grandma. "That's a lot."

"But it includes everything," said Morgan. "Transportation, equipment rental, lift tickets, food, and everything for three whole days! Janna said it would cost more if we weren't going as a group."

"That's probably true," said Mom as they piled into the car. "Lift tickets alone are pretty expensive."

"And the church is offering ways for kids to earn money to go," continued Morgan.

"Like what?" asked Mom.

"We can make stuff to sell at the bazaar."

"That's less than two weeks from now," said Grandma.

"And Cory and Janna are going to cut down Christmas trees to sell. We can help with that too," said Morgan.

"And wreath making," added Emily in a slightly flat voice.

"Sounds like you girls are going to be busy," said Grandma.

"Does that mean I can go?" asked Morgan.

"I guess so," said Mom, "if you're sure you can earn the money. You know that things are kind of tight right now."

"I know," Morgan assured her. "And I plan on trusting God to provide."

"How about you, Emily?" asked Grandma.

"You mean, am I trusting God too?" Emily sighed.

Grandma laughed. "Oh, I know you're trusting God, sweetheart. But how about the ski trip — are you planning on going too?"

"I don't know … that's a lot of money."

"But our God is a big God," Morgan reminded her. "We can expect big things from him."

"How many kids are going?" asked Mom.

"I don't know," admitted Morgan. "But Cory said we could invite friends from outside of church. We're going to invite Carlie, Amy, and Chelsea."

"We are?" Emily's brow creased. "Since when?"

"Since now," said Morgan. "Or when we get home. We have a meeting today at two."

"And you're inviting them to go on the ski trip?" asked Emily.

"Of course," said Morgan. "How much fun would it be without them?"

"Well, I hope you have fun without me."

"Oh, Emily, don't be so negative."

"And don't be so bossy, Morgan," warned Mom. "Emily needs to talk to her mom about this before she commits to anything."

"I know …" Morgan told herself to calm down. "It's just that I'm so excited about it. It's going to be so cool."

"You barely know how to ski," Mom reminded her.

"Janna said she'd give ski lessons. And Cory said he'd teach kids to snowboard. We can pick whichever one we want, but we have to tell them when we sign up."

"When do you sign up?" asked Mom.

"As soon as possible," said Morgan.

"As soon as God provides some of us with fifty dollars," added Emily.

"Fifty dollars?" echoed Grandma.

"Yeah, that's the deposit," explained Morgan. "I have fifteen now, Mom. If you loan me the rest, I can pay you back as soon as I earn it. And I already have some bead necklaces to sell at the bazaar."

"We'll talk about it at home, Morgan."

Morgan turned to Emily. "You *are* going on this ski trip, Em. I can just feel it. God wants to show you that he is a lot bigger than you think."

"God owns the cattle on a thousand hills," said Grandma. "And a whole lot more, Emily. Morgan is right. If God wants you to go, he will provide."

"What's your family doing for Thanksgiving this week, Emily?" asked Mom as she turned into Harbor View Mobile-Home Court.

"Nothing that I know of," said Emily as she reached for her bag.

"Why don't you come to our house for dinner?" said Grandma.

"Yeah," agreed Morgan. "Grandma makes the best pies, and her cornbread stuffing is awesome."

"That's a great idea," said Mom as she pulled in front of Emily's house. "We'd love to have you join us."

"I'll check with my mom," said Emily as she opened the door. Then she thanked them for the ride and got out.

Morgan felt a small wave of guilt as she watched Emily slowly walking toward her house. She could tell that Emily was discouraged, and Morgan hoped that she hadn't come on too strong about the ski trip. Two hundred dollars really was a lot of money; and it probably did seem overwhelming to Emily. Especially this time of year when things slowed down at the resort where Emily's mom worked. Finances might be tougher than usual for their family. Still, Morgan felt certain that the money dilemma would be resolved — the girls would work hard and God would help them. She just needed to convince Emily.

"Go easy on Emily, Morgan," said Mom as she pulled into their driveway.

"What do you mean?"

"I mean there's a chance that Emily's mom won't want her to go on that ski trip. Lisa told me just the other day that she was thinking about getting a second job during the winter."

"But Emily and I can earn our money, Mom. We can make things and sell Christmas trees and whatever it takes."

"Lisa might need Emily to help out more at home," said Mom in a slightly warning tone. "I just don't want you to put too much pressure on Emily."

"But she has to go on the ski trip," insisted Morgan. "It wouldn't be the same without her."

"That's not for you to say, sweetheart," said Grandma. "But if you pray about it, maybe God will make a way for Emily to go."

Morgan just nodded as they walked up to the house. But sometimes she wondered why other people didn't have the same kind of faith she had — the kind of faith where you were willing to stand up and speak out. At least she thought it was faith — she hoped it was faith. And, unless God showed her otherwise, she'd continue to believe that it was faith. In the meantime, she'd be praying really hard for Emily to go on the ski trip.

Morgan went to her room and started going through her bead box. Her beading supplies were a little low at the moment. She had several necklaces partially done, as well as enough beads to create a bracelet or two. Still, even if she sold all of them, it would probably be barely enough to cover her deposit and certainly not enough for Emily too. Besides that, the church bazaar was almost two weeks away — what if the ski trip filled up before then? What else could she do to earn money?

She looked around her room. She had some sewing projects going, but they weren't the sorts of things you could sell at a bazaar. She also had some watercolor paintings that she'd been working on, but she wasn't so sure that anyone would want to buy them. She wasn't even sure she'd be willing to have them hanging on a wall for people to gawk at. Art was still a somewhat personal thing to her.

"Morgan," called Grandma. "Come eat lunch." As they were eating, Morgan told Mom and Grandma that she was short on beads and was wondering if there was anything else she could make to sell at the bazaar.

"I'm knitting things for the bazaar," said Grandma. "But it takes time to knit."

"And I'm not a fast knitter at all," said Morgan, but she didn't admit that she really didn't like to knit. She didn't want to hurt Grandma's feelings.

"I have an idea," said Grandma as they were finishing up. "You could make socks."

Morgan frowned. "Socks? You mean by knitting?"

"No. I got a sewing pattern in the mail a couple of months ago. It's for polar fleece socks."

Morgan brightened. "Like for skiing and snow and stuff?"

"Yes, I suppose ..." said Grandma. "Generally, I thought they'd be for keeping your feet warm."

"Weren't you going to make some of those to sell in my shop?" asked Mom.

"Yes, but I just haven't gotten around to it."

"Do they look hard to make?" asked Morgan.

"No, I don't think so. They may involve a bit of cutting. But the sewing looked like it would be simple enough ... if you follow the directions." Grandma winked at Morgan.

"I can follow directions," said Morgan as she set down her milk glass. "It's just that I sometimes like doing things *my way*."

"Well, that works for some projects, but I suspect the socks need to be sewn a particular way."

"Can I try making some?"

"Of course. I even have a bit of polar fleece for you to practice on. It's that tiger stripe that's leftover from the throw I made for your room."

"Cool."

"No," said Grandma. "*Warm.*"

"Right." Morgan thanked Grandma for lunch as well as the sock idea then looked up at the kitchen clock. "I gotta go unlock the clubhouse before the others get there," she said as she stood. "I want to invite everyone to the ski trip."

"Just remember," said Mom. "Two hundred dollars is a lot of money. Don't make anyone feel bad if they can't afford to go."

Morgan gave her mom a wounded expression. "*Mom,*" she said, "I would *never* do that. They're my friends. I don't want them to feel bad. I just want them to have enough faith so that we can all go and have a really awesome time."

Grandma laughed. "Don't worry, Cleo," she said to her daughter as Morgan headed for the front door. "I think Morgan has enough faith for all five of those girls."

"That may be so," called Mom. "But, Morgan, it's a deluge out there. Put on your rain slicker before you go out. I don't think you have enough faith to stay dry in that downpour."

Morgan grabbed her bright orange slicker and went outside. Mom was right. There was a regular monsoon going on. She stood on the porch for a moment, just watching the rain careening down the gutters like waterfalls. She peered across the way to Emily's house, also shrouded in rain. In need of paint and some other repairs, Emily's house was the most rundown of the mobile homes in their park. But then Emily's mom was only renting and couldn't afford to fix it up much. Morgan knew that Mrs. Adams didn't get any child support and had a hard time making ends meet. Then there was Carlie's family on the other side of the beach trail. Their house was in better shape, but only because Mr. Garcia was a hard worker. Still, with their three kids to support, Morgan knew that it probably wasn't easy for them either. Maybe Mom and Grandma were right. Maybe it was silly of Morgan to think that all the girls in their club could afford to go on the ski trip with her. The truth was Morgan wasn't even sure that she could earn two hundred dollars in a month's time. Maybe it was just a crazy notion.

Then Morgan thought about what time of year it was — late November. She usually made gifts for her family and friends during December. What if she was so busy trying to earn money for a ski trip that she had nothing to give? Wasn't it selfish to think only of herself right now? All these troubling thoughts ran through her mind as she jogged down the sandy beach trail, jumping over pond-sized puddles, as she made her way to the old bus that served as their clubhouse. Even as she turned the key on the door of the beloved rainbow bus, she didn't feel a bit encouraged — instead of its usual bright and cheerful colors, thanks to the gray clouds, the bus looked dull and dowdy today. Then, just as Morgan stepped on the stair to go inside, a whoosh of rainwater slid off the sloped roof and splashed down onto her head.

She shuddered and went inside, closing the door behind her. She peeled off her coat and dried off her glasses. Maybe it was the gloomy weather, or maybe it was her mother's warnings, but it suddenly felt as if Morgan's faith was shrinking — and shrinking fast.

chapter two

"Let's call this meeting to order," said Morgan as the girls all chattered away as usual. Their wet raincoats were piled up at the front of the bus, and the insides of the windows were already steamed up from all the moisture. Morgan had turned on the little heater as well as the strings of colorful lights that she'd gotten at the gift show last summer, but even this didn't seem to be lifting her spirits. Emily, the secretary, went over the minutes of their last meeting, which, as usual, took just a couple of minutes. Then Amy said she had an announcement.

"Miss McPhearson has invited us to her house for a post-Thanksgiving tea," said Amy with her usual authority. "She'd like us to join her at three o'clock on the Saturday following Thanksgiving. Does that work for everyone?"

"Not me," said Chelsea. "Our family is going on a ski trip for Thanksgiving. I'll be gone until Sunday."

"Lucky duck," said Amy.

"That's not all," said Chelsea. "I just found out that my dad got me a really great new snowboard. He was going to save it till Christmas, but Mom said that he'll probably let me have it early and—"

"*You* know how to snowboard?" asked Carlie.

"Mostly I know how to ski," said Chelsea. "But my brother promised to teach me, and he's a really good rider."

"What's a rider?" asked Carlie.

"A snowboarder, silly," said Chelsea. "You didn't know that?"

"Maybe …" Carlie shrugged. "I guess I might've forgot or something."

"Well, speaking of skiing and snowboarding," said Emily. "Morgan was going to tell—"

"Wait a minute," yelled Amy. "I'm not done with *my* business yet. I need to know who can go to Miss McPhearson's house for tea." She glared at the girls. "Hands, please."

Morgan, Carlie, and Emily raised their hands.

"Thank you." Amy pushed a strand of black hair away from her eyes. "I will let Miss McPhearson know ASAP."

"Okay," said Emily, "Morgan wanted to—"

"Wait a minute," demanded Amy again. "You haven't asked for the treasurer's report."

"Oh, yeah," said Emily. She rolled her eyes. "I'm sure it's changed a lot since last week."

"It's proper procedure," said Amy. Then she read the amount in the treasury fund and frowned. "I was thinking we should either start having dues or do something to earn money."

"Why?" asked Emily.

"In case something comes up," said Amy. "Like when we did the park project. It would've helped us to get started if we'd had a little more cash on hand."

"But it worked out," said Carlie.

"I know," said Amy. "But as a responsible treasurer, I feel it's my duty to encourage our club to be financially fiscal."

"Financially fiscal?" Morgan frowned at Amy. "What do you mean? We're not a business."

"We're sort of like a business."

"Oh, Amy," said Chelsea. "Give it a rest, will ya?"

"Yeah," agreed Emily. "Now Morgan has something to tell us." Emily turned and looked at Morgan.

"Oh, I don't know …" Morgan wasn't sure she wanted to make her announcement now.

"What's wrong?" asked Emily. "I thought you were going to invite everyone —"

"I don't know if it's such a good idea now." Morgan tried to give Emily a look — a look that was supposed to say "I don't want to talk about this now." But Emily obviously wasn't getting it.

"Hey," said Chelsea. "What's the deal, Morgan? First you're going to invite us to something, and then you change your mind and un-invite us?"

"That's not very polite," added Amy.

"Yeah," said Carlie. "What's up with that, Morgan?"

"Fine, fine," said Morgan, holding up her hands. "I'll tell you. I was going to ask everyone here if you wanted to go on a ski trip with our youth group. It's the week after Christmas, it's for three days and —"

"All right!" said Carlie, giving Chelsea a high five. "I'm in."

"Me too," said Chelsea. "I can't wait to show you guys my new board."

"I'd like to come too," said Amy. "I've never skied before, but I'd like to try."

"How about you, Emily?" asked Carlie. "You're coming too, right?"

Emily looked down at her lap. "I don't know …"

"Why not?" demanded Amy.

Emily looked up now, her eyes on Morgan. "Tell them," she said. "Tell them how much it costs."

"Well, I was about to …" Morgan adjusted her glasses and looked at her friends. "But then I got interrupted. Anyway, the trip, which includes transportation, lift tickets, equipment rental, food, and lodging … is two hundred dollars."

"That's not bad," said Chelsea. "Count me in."

"Whoa," said Carlie. "I don't know about that …"

"It's a good deal," said Chelsea. "Seriously, I heard my mom saying how much our weekend is costing us — trust me, two hundred dollars a person is not bad."

"Maybe for you," said Carlie. "But I don't have that kind of money."

"Two hundred dollars?" said Amy in a thoughtful voice.

"Yeah," said Morgan. "Is that too much for you too?"

"No …" Amy slowly shook her head. "I think I can afford that. My parents have been paying me for helping in the restaurant lately. And I'll work a lot during the holidays. Plus, tips are supposed to be good during December. I'll go."

"Not me," said Carlie sadly.

"So, I'm not so sure," said Morgan. "I've been having second thoughts about the whole thing. Maybe we should make some kind of pact. Either we all go, or none of us go."

"That's not fair," said Amy.

"Well, I don't know if I want to go …" began Morgan. "I mean, if Emily and Carlie can't go too. It just wouldn't feel right to me. It wouldn't be fun. Maybe we should just forget it."

"Wait," said Emily. "You didn't tell them everything, Morgan." She turned to Carlie now. "Our church has ways for kids to earn money."

"But I don't go to your church," said Carlie.

"I don't think that matters," said Emily. "The youth pastor said we could invite our friends." Then she told the others about the Christmas bazaar and selling Christmas trees and wreathes.

"Really?" said Carlie hopefully. "We could do that?"

"But two hundred dollars is a lot of money," Morgan pointed out. "And there's not much time. And anyone who goes needs to pay a deposit of fifty dollars, and I'm guessing that needs to be paid pretty soon. Plus, don't forget it's Christmas ... it can get pretty busy, you know."

Carlie frowned. "Maybe you're right ... maybe I better not try to do this."

"Hang on," said Emily. "You can't give up that easily."

Morgan stared at her friend in surprise. "But I didn't think you were going to go, Emily."

"I never said that."

"But you worried about the cost."

"Yeah, and you kept telling me to have bigger faith. What happened to your faith, Morgan?"

Morgan blinked. "I still have it. I just didn't want to be too pushy ... in case some of us couldn't go."

"Well, I'm not ready to give up," said Emily with a stubborn smile.

"Really?" Morgan felt a trickle of hope again.

"Me neither," said Carlie. "I might even see if I can do some babysitting for my mom again. There's a whole week of no school right before Christmas. My mom might pay me to watch my little brothers so that she can get some things done before Christmas."

"So, it's settled?" asked Morgan, still feeling surprised.

"Everyone who wants to go on the ski trip, raise your hand," said Amy.

Everyone's hand, except Morgan's, shot into the air. Then Morgan sheepishly raised her own hand.

"This is going to be so cool," said Carlie. "I can't wait."

"I'll get the sign-up forms for everyone tomorrow," said Morgan. "I'll bring them to the clubhouse after school."

"When do we pay our deposit?" asked Amy.

Morgan considered this. "I guess whenever you can."

"I'll bring a check for the whole thing tomorrow," said Chelsea.

Morgan nodded. "Okay …" But even as she said this, she wondered whether the check could be refunded if things didn't work out. Cory hadn't said anything about that. But it might be pretty weird if Chelsea was the only one to come up with the full payment for the ski trip — and she had to go all by herself. Of course, Chelsea would probably refuse to go alone. And her parents probably wouldn't even care if she didn't get her money back. Morgan couldn't imagine how it would feel to be that rich.

"Will boys be there?" asked Chelsea suddenly.

"Boys?" Morgan considered this. "Well, yeah, sure. The youth group is both guys and girls."

"What are we going to wear?" asked Carlie. And that's when Chelsea started giving them fashion tips on winter wear.

"I'll bring some magazines," said Chelsea. "That'll give you guys some ideas of what's cool right now and what's not."

"That reminds me," said Morgan. "My grandma has a pattern for socks."

"Huh?" said Chelsea.

"Polar socks," continued Morgan. "We can sew them and sell them at the bazaar."

Chelsea frowned. "You're going to *sew* socks?"

"Yeah, I think so," said Morgan. "I'm going to experiment with it. See how long it takes, how much the fabric costs … and if it seems profitable or not."

"Hey, I'm not too proud to sew socks," said Emily.

"Me neither," said Carlie.

Chelsea shrugged. "It might even be fun."

"I don't know," said Amy. "I think I better stick with waiting tables for now."

"I'll practice with the sock pattern," said Morgan. "And if it works, we can set up a workshop here at the bus. The church bazaar is less than two weeks away. We don't have any time to waste."

"Speaking of two weeks from now," said Chelsea. "My dad told me to see if you guys want to be in the Christmas parade."

"Doing what?" asked Amy with suspicion.

"Just riding on the bank float," said Chelsea, and then she giggled. "Dressed as elves."

"Elves?" Carlie frowned. "Like tights and pointy shoes?"

"Yeah. Dad will provide the costumes."

"I think it sounds like fun," said Morgan. "I'll volunteer to be an elf."

"What about the church bazaar?" asked Emily. "Isn't it the same day?"

"I don't think we actually have to be at the bazaar," said Morgan. "I bet we just have to get our stuff there and set things up. My grandma does the bazaar every year and she usually just works a few hours, not all day."

"So, it's set?" asked Chelsea. "Five elves for Daddy's float?"

"Does he pay?" asked Amy.

Chelsea laughed. "Are you kidding? My dad thinks we should all be honored just to ride on his precious float. But I can probably talk him into lunch afterward."

"It's a date," said Carlie.

So it was settled. The five girls would play Santa's elves in the parade and then work like elves the rest of the time. Morgan just hoped that there would be enough time to do everything. She knew that it wasn't up to her to make sure that this all worked out, but she couldn't help but feel somewhat responsible. Mostly she didn't want to see any of the girls lose money on the ski trip. Well, besides Chelsea … and only because she could afford it.

The rain had almost completely stopped by the time the group started to break up. Amy had to leave early to help at her parents' restaurant. Chelsea had to go because her mom was picking her up, and Carlie had to get home to help her mom watch the boys. Then it was just Emily and Morgan.

"Did you mind what I said?" asked Emily as they were putting on their raincoats.

"About what?"

"You know … about all of us going on the ski trip. I saw you giving me the evil eye."

"I guess I was just surprised. I was ready to give it up and just forget it."

"After your big speech about faith?"

"I just wasn't sure whether I was having faith in God or faith in Morgan."

Emily laughed. "Maybe it was both."

"I just hope it works out."

"Sure, it will," said Emily. "We'll be praying about it, won't we?"

"Of course." Morgan glanced at Emily. "What made you change your mind like that? I mean, this morning you seemed so sure that you couldn't make enough money to go … and now you're all cool with it."

"I got to thinking about Cory and Janna …"

"Huh?"

"I was just thinking about how much I've learned in youth group these past several months … and I thought maybe Amy, Chelsea, and Carlie would like to be around them for a while too. I mean, not to recruit them into our church or anything …"

"I get it," said Morgan as she locked the bus door.

"Is that weird?"

Morgan shook her head. "No, that is very cool." She smiled at Emily. "I think your faith is bigger than mine."

"No way," said Emily.

"Way."

"Hey, I asked my mom about going to your house for Thanksgiving … and you know what she told me?"

"No."

"She said she'd love to come, except that she already invited Mr. Greeley to come to our house for Thanksgiving."

"Really?" Morgan tried to imagine old Mr. Greeley sitting at the kitchen table with Emily, her mom, and her sixteen-year-old brother, Kyle.

"Pretty weird, huh?"

"No … I mean Mr. Greeley is a nice old guy. And I know he really likes you and your family, Em."

"Still, it'll be sort of odd … I mean he's not exactly talkative. And Kyle is still kind of afraid of him."

"That's just because he doesn't know him." Morgan remembered how she used to be afraid of strange Mr. Greeley too — back before he gave them the keys to their clubhouse. "I know!" said Morgan suddenly. "Why don't you guys just bring Mr. Greeley over to our house for Thanksgiving? You know, the more the merrier."

"That sounds good to me. I'll check with Mom and get back to you."

"Hopefully, you guys can come. I have it all planned out," said Morgan. "I should have figured out the socks by then, and you and I can get a head start by cutting out a bunch of them."

"And can I sew them too?"

"Sure," said Morgan. "You were doing really good on my sewing machine when we made the pillows and stuff for the bus."

"Cool." Emily gave her a high five. "And I'm so excited about the ski trip. It's going to be awesome!"

Morgan hugged Emily. "I'm so glad you changed your mind about the ski trip," she said happily. "I guess my faith was starting to shrink. I think I would've given up on the trip if you hadn't said something just when you did."

Emily grinned. "Guess that's what friends are for, huh?"

Morgan thought about that as she walked home. It was hard to remember what life had been like before Emily moved here last spring. It seemed like they'd been friends forever, but in reality it had only been about six months, give or take. Still, Morgan knew that theirs was a friendship that would last forever. And if for some reason Emily was unable to go on the ski trip, Morgan would gladly forfeit her spot as well. She wouldn't care if it was completely paid for, or if all the other girls were going. Morgan would stay home with Emily.

She just hoped it wouldn't come down to that. And she'd be praying extra hard to make sure that it didn't!

chapter three

"I'm so bummed," said Carlie as the four friends walked to school on Monday.

"What's up?" asked Amy.

"Chelsea called me last night — I couldn't believe it — she invited me to go with her and her family to the ski resort."

"Wow," said Emily. "That sounds awesome."

"Yeah," agreed Morgan, "Why are you bummed about that?"

Carlie kicked a stone off the sidewalk. "Because my parents said 'no way, José.'"

"Why?" asked Emily.

"Because it's Thanksgiving," said Carlie. "My parents are so old-fashioned. They think the world will come to an end if all of our family — I mean aunts and uncles and cousins and everyone — isn't together under one roof for that entire day."

"That's kind of nice," said Morgan. "I can't imagine having that much family around."

Carlie let out a long sigh. "Yeah, there's like eighty people. They all come to my aunt's house, which usually seems pretty roomy, but it's so crowded in there you can hardly breathe. And noisy? Have you ever been to a Latino celebration? Man, your ears are ringing for three days afterward."

The girls laughed.

"Well, my parents are old-fashioned too," said Amy. "But not about holidays. For my parents, the holidays are just a time to make money in the restaurant. I'll be working on Thanksgiving."

"Really?" asked Emily. "Do very many people eat Chinese food on Thanksgiving?"

"You'd be surprised," said Amy. "I think most of our holiday customers don't have family around. But at least they're generous with their tips. Even so, I'd give anything to have Carlie's problem. I wish Chelsea would invite me to go skiing with her."

"Maybe she will," said Carlie sadly.

They were almost at Boscoe Bay Middle School now.

"Well, cheer up," said Emily, "At least you have the ski trip after Christmas to look forward to."

"Yeah," said Carlie. "After my parents nixed my chances of going with Chelsea, I asked about the ski trip, and it sounded like it might be okay. My mom even agreed to pay me to watch the boys while she gets ready for Christmas, and my dad offered to help us to go cut down Christmas trees to sell at the bazaar."

"That's great," said Morgan. "Maybe that whole thing with Chelsea helped to soften them up."

Carlie laughed. "Yeah, that's what I was thinking too."

"Speaking of Chelsea," said Amy, pointing to the Mercedes that was just pulling up in front of the school. "There she is."

"Hey, Chelsea," called Carlie, waving.

Chelsea came over to join them as they went up the steps to the front entrance. "I'm still mad at you," Chelsea said to Carlie with a pouting face.

Carlie shrugged. "Hey, I can't help what my parents say."

"At least we still have the ski trip to look forward to after Christmas," Morgan reminded her. "I'm going to pick up the forms today."

"I already have my deposit money," said Amy. "It's at home, but I counted it out last night and I have just enough."

"And my dad will give me a check for the whole thing," said Chelsea.

"And I was just telling these guys that my parents said I can go to that — since it's not actually on Christmas," said Carlie as they went inside the school. "My mom even offered to advance me some babysitting money so I can pay the deposit."

Emily glanced at Morgan with an uneasy expression as they walked to their lockers. Morgan could tell that she was still a little worried about the money. But Morgan smiled at her in a way she hoped was reassuring.

"It's going to be so cool," Morgan said to her friends. "All five of us up there, skiing and riding and having a totally great time."

"I think I want to try snowboarding," said Carlie.

"Yeah, and I should be pretty good at it by then," added Chelsea.

"I'm going to ski," said Amy. "I think it looks more graceful."

"Snowboarding's more fun," said Emily.

"How do *you* know?" Amy asked her.

"Because I've done it."

Morgan blinked. "You've gone snowboarding before, Emily?"

"Yeah, when we lived in Idaho." Emily got a worried look now, and Morgan knew that it was because she didn't like to mention where they'd moved from. "I mean when we were in Idaho ... we went a few times."

"Have you been to Sun Valley?" asked Chelsea.

"No," said Emily. "Not to ride anyway. We went there once just to check it out."

"My sister has been there. She says it's awesome."

Just then the warning bell rang, and the girls scattered off toward their first-period classes. But as Morgan and Emily went to English, Morgan had to ask. "You've really been snowboarding before?"

"Yeah, I thought I told you."

"No." Morgan shook her head. "Are you any good?"

Emily shrugged. "Not the first time … but I kinda got the hang of it. It's not that hard, really. And you're pretty athletic, Morgan, so you shouldn't have any problem. Have you ever skateboarded?"

"No."

"Oh." Emily grinned. "My brother taught me to skateboard when I was like six. I could probably borrow Kyle's board and give you some lessons. It's all about balance."

"All right," said Morgan as they took their seats. Then as Mrs. Robertson began to drone on about punctuation and sentence structure, Morgan began to daydream about snowboarding down a white snowy peak. Naturally, she was able to do this with grace and style. And, Morgan realized, in her daydream her hair was loose and flowing. Maybe it was time to lose the beaded braids. Morgan fingered a braid. Her hair was past her shoulders now. She wondered what it would look like without the braids. Perhaps she could get the curl relaxed a little, the way her mother did.

"Morgan Evans?" A shrill voice interrupted her daydreaming.

Morgan adjusted her glasses and looked up at Mrs. Robertson who was looking directly at Morgan.

"Can you tell me ... does this sentence require a semi-colon or a comma?"

Morgan studied the sentence that Mrs. Robertson was pointing to on the board. She had no idea which was the right answer, but since there was a fifty-fifty chance, she decided to guess. "A comma."

"No," said Mrs. Robertson crisply. "And if you had been listening, you would've known that this particular sentence requires a semicolon," and then she went on to explain the reason why. Although, even as Morgan listened, she wasn't so sure she got it. Why wouldn't a comma work just as well? Just the same, this little embarrassment was a good reminder that she needed to pay attention. Daydreaming was okay when you weren't at school, but Morgan knew that it would be a mistake to get behind in class.

At noon, Morgan went to their regular table in the cafeteria. As usual, Morgan had a sack lunch from home. And, as usual, she and Carlie and Amy were the first ones at their table. This was because the three of them usually brought lunches from home. Morgan felt like they were the lucky ones. Amy mostly brought food from the restaurant. Carlie usually had something that smelled delightfully Mexican. And Morgan had whatever Grandma had decided she needed for that day. Morgan knew that Emily ate the cafeteria food for two reasons. One reason was top secret: because Emily was entitled to vouchers. Fortunately, their school's vouchers looked exactly like regular lunch tickets. The other reason was because Emily's mother wasn't much into cooking. The reason Chelsea ate cafeteria food was a mystery. But Chelsea claimed she liked it. For the most part, Chelsea ate the same thing everyday — salad and diet soda. Morgan didn't think it was the most healthy or even appetizing meal, but she had learned early on that it was better not to mention this to Chelsea.

"You are not going to believe this," said Emily as she and Chelsea sat down to join them.

"What?" asked Morgan.

"Chelsea invited *me* to go to the resort with her and her family."

"No way," said Amy with a disappointed frown. "Why didn't you ask me, Chelsea?"

Chelsea shrugged. "I thought you had to work, Amy."

"I would've gotten out of it." Amy scowled. "I suppose this means that only Morgan, Carlie, and I will be going to Miss McPhearson's tea now."

"Sorry to miss that," said Emily. "Tell her hello for me, okay?"

"But why Emily?" demanded Amy, still unwilling to give it up. "You guys aren't even that good of friends."

"For one thing, Emily actually knows how to snowboard." Chelsea stuck a straw in her soda. "So she was kinda ahead of the game after Carlie dropped out."

"I am so jealous," said Carlie.

"I'm sorry," said Emily. "If you could've gone I wouldn't — "

"That's okay," said Carlie. She smiled at Chelsea now. "I'm glad you have someone to go with you."

Chelsea nodded. "Yeah, that'll make it more fun."

Morgan just stared at Emily. Was she honestly planning on going with Chelsea? Those two didn't even get along that well. "How do you even know you can go yet, Emily?" she asked as she opened a plastic bag and removed half a sandwich.

"I let her use my phone," said Chelsea. "She already called her mom at work."

"And Mom said it was fine."

Morgan wanted to ask her what this meant about Thanksgiving. Were Emily's mom and brother and Mr. Greeley still coming to Morgan's house? But she couldn't think of a way to say it without sounding mad. Instead, she just focused on her lunch. Meanwhile, the other girls chattered away about snowboarding and clothes and most of it went right over Morgan's head.

By the end of the day, Morgan knew that she was jealous. But she also knew that she didn't want anyone to know. As usual, the five girls met at their lockers.

"It's weird not having soccer to go to," said Chelsea as she closed her locker.

"And basketball doesn't start up until after Christmas," said Carlie.

"Well, I'm going to go by the church and pick up the forms for the ski trip," said Morgan. "If anyone wants to get one, they'll be at the clubhouse."

"Do you need a ride?" asked Chelsea. "My mom's picking me up."

Morgan considered this. On one hand she felt sort of mad at Chelsea right now … but on the other hand, it was a quite a walk to the other end of town to get to the church and then all the way back home again. "Sure," she told Chelsea. "That'd be nice."

"Anyone else?" offered Chelsea.

"I have to go to the restaurant," said Amy. "Work, work, work … all I do is work."

Emily laughed. "Yeah, right. I've seen how busy it is at the restaurant this time of day. You and your sisters and brother usually watch TV and eat."

Amy made a face, then laughed. "Well, I can complain if I want to."

"And I have to get home to watch my brothers," said Carlie. "Mom and Tia Maria are getting a head start on Thanksgiving shopping. But at least I'll be earning money for the ski trip."

Then Carlie and Amy left to walk home together.

"How about you, Emily?" asked Chelsea. "Want a ride?"

"Sounds good."

So the three of them went out to wait for Chelsea's mom. As they waited, Chelsea and Emily discussed what Emily would need to bring on Thursday. Morgan pretended to be distracted with a sketch she was creating on the front of her notebook. It was a tiger, partially hidden behind a tree.

"You can borrow my old ski pants," said Chelsea. "In fact, you can have them. I don't need them anymore."

"Cool," said Emily. "What color are they?"

"They're just navy blue, but they are Tommy Hilfiger," said Chelsea. "In fact, you can have the jacket that goes with them too. It's a little tight on me anyway, and I don't think you're as big on top as I am."

"Bragging again, are you?" teased Emily.

Chelsea laughed. *"We all develop at different rates,"* she said in a voice that Morgan knew was an imitation of their health teacher, Miss Perrell.

"Yes," said Emily in the same tone. *"And we do not make fun of others just because their bodies are different than ours."*

"There's my mom," said Chelsea.

Soon all three were in Chelsea's car. "I told Morgan we'd give her a lift to her church so she can get the stuff for the ski trip."

"That's fine," said Mrs. Landers. "Hello, Emily and Morgan. I haven't seen you two since the park project.

How's it going?"

"Okay," said Morgan in a slightly flat tone.

"Good," said Emily. "Thanks."

"Guess what, Mom?"

"What?"

"Emily is going to come with us to the resort for Thanksgiving."

"That's wonderful. I was just feeling sad that you wouldn't have a friend up there. Meredith and Jason are each bringing someone." She glanced at Emily. "Are your parents okay with that? Do I need to call them or anything?"

"She just has a mom," said Chelsea in a quiet voice.

"Yes, that's right. I knew that. Is your mother all right with you going?"

"Yeah," said Emily. "Chelsea let me call my mom on her cell phone. And it's okay. I mean, as long as Mom knows where we'll be and phone numbers and all that sort of thing."

"I'll write it all out," said Mrs. Landers. "Chelsea can bring it to school tomorrow. And your mom can call me if she has any questions."

Morgan kept her eyes on her drawing of the tiger. But as she filled in the stripes, she felt seriously jealous and angry. Plus, she kept asking herself, why hadn't she simply walked to the church? The exercise probably would've helped with her attitude — and she wouldn't have been subjected to all this.

"You can just drop me off at the church, Mrs. Landers," said Morgan in voice that sounded much brighter than she felt. Still, she thought this might be a way to escape the little happy party going on between Chelsea and Emily right now.

"Don't you want a ride back home?" asked Chelsea.

"No, I need to talk to Pastor George about something," Morgan told them, although that wasn't completely true. But she would make it true. She would go and tell Pastor George about her jealousy fit, and perhaps he would straighten her out. It seemed like a good plan. "I can just walk home afterward."

"Well, if you're sure," said Mrs. Landers as she pulled up in front of the church.

"Yes," said Morgan. "And the exercise will do me good."

"But while we're here," said Mrs. Landers, "Why don't I just make out a check for the ski trip. Then it will be all taken care of."

"Works for me," said Chelsea. "I'll go in with Morgan and get the form while you write the check."

"I'll go in too," said Emily.

So the three of them went into the church office together, where Chelsea and Emily each picked up their own forms and Morgan got three.

"I'm going to take this out to my mom to fill out," said Chelsea after Morgan introduced her to the church secretary.

"At this rate, it looks like you're going to fill up the whole ski trip, Morgan," said Mrs. Albert. "Cory and Janna should be pleased."

Morgan folded the papers and slipped them into her backpack. "I don't think I can fill up the whole ski trip, Mrs. Albert. Just five spots … for me and my friends."

"Well, good for you." Mrs. Albert smiled. "And you're going too, Emily?"

"I hope so," said Emily.

Morgan was about to ask if Pastor George was around, but then realized that it could pose a problem to her escape plan if he wasn't there right now. So she decided to just chat with Mrs. Albert. "We're going to be making things for the bazaar," she said. "And our friend Carlie's dad is going to help us cut down Christmas trees, and we'll make wreaths and things to sell so that we can earn our way for the ski trip."

"Sounds like you girls have a busy month ahead."

Just then Chelsea reappeared with her completed form and check. "Here you go," she told Mrs. Albert. "All set."

"Well, we've had a few deposits, but you're the first one to be paid in full, Chelsea. Thank you."

"No problem," said Chelsea. "Ready to roll, Em?"

"See ya later, Morgan," called Emily.

"Yeah," said Chelsea. "Later."

Then Morgan was alone in the office with Mrs. Albert. She felt embarrassed and slightly abandoned, and wasn't even sure that she really wanted to talk to Pastor George now.

"Was there something else you needed, dear?" asked Mrs. Albert.

"No," said Morgan. She felt a lump growing in her throat.

"Why didn't you leave with your friends?"

"I ... uh ... I wanted to walk home," she said, blinking back tears.

"Oh ..."

Then Morgan said good-bye and turned and slowly made her way to the front door. She wanted to be sure that the Mercedes was completely out of sight. It was. So she went out and began walking back toward home. Alone. The lump in her throat was growing bigger, and the breeze off the ocean was picking up. And, before long, the wind began to chill the tears that had sneaked down her cheeks.

chapter four

"Are you mad at me?" Emily asked Morgan on Wednesday.

"No, of course not," said Morgan. The two of them were in the clubhouse, getting ready for the others to arrive for a quick Thanksgiving party that Amy had insisted they needed to have. Although Amy, at the moment, was nowhere to be seen.

"But you've been acting different," said Emily.

"Different than what?" asked Morgan as she set out napkins and paper cups.

"Different like you're mad or something."

Morgan turned to face Emily now. Maybe it was time to be honest. "I guess I'm hurt," she said.

"Because I'm going with Chelsea?"

Morgan shrugged. "I'd been looking forward to you coming over for Thanksgiving ... I thought we were going to work on the polar socks."

"But we can do that next week," said Emily.

"I know, but ..."

Just then Amy walked in carrying a pink box. "Happy Thanksgiving," she said as she set the box on the table. "I made these myself."

"Ooh, those are pretty," said Emily as Amy opened the box to display cupcakes frosted in shades of yellow, orange, and gold and topped with candy corn.

"Chocolate," said Amy. "And see how I tinted the frosting different colors?"

"These are really nice," said Morgan.

"Here come Chelsea and Carlie," said Emily, pointing out the window.

"Happy Thanksgiving," said Chelsea as she set down a grocery bag. "I brought chips and soda."

"I'll put some music on," offered Emily, going over to the old-fashioned record player and selecting a vinyl record.

Soon the five of them were eating and laughing and talking, and Morgan began to feel a little bit better, telling herself that it was just like old times. She knew she shouldn't be so bummed about the fact that Emily was going to do something with Chelsea. All five of them were friends. And it was okay to do things with different people. Maybe she'd invite Carlie and Amy over during the weekend to work on socks. Morgan knew that jealousy was a sin. And she was going to do everything she could to get over it.

"The elf costumes for the Christmas parade arrived," said Chelsea. "And I hate to admit it, but they're pretty geeky looking." She made a face. "I thought maybe we could rework them somehow since we don't want to look like freaks up there on the float." She pointed at Morgan. "You're pretty good at that sort of thing. Maybe you can think of a way to make them look cool."

"Sure," said Morgan.

"Let's plan on getting together next week then." Chelsea looked at her watch and then at Emily. "Uh-oh, Em, we gotta go. My mom is probably already at your house by now."

"But it's not even five," said Morgan.

"I know. We're supposed to be on the road at five," said Chelsea. "They have this big dinner at the lodge tonight, with live music and everything. We don't wanna be late."

"Sorry we can't stay to clean up," said Emily as Chelsea tugged her by the arm. "You guys have a good Thanksgiving."

"You too," called Amy.

"Don't break any bones," added Carlie.

"Have fun," said Morgan, although her heart was not in it.

"I have to go too," said Amy. "The restaurant is calling..."

"Me too," said Carlie. "I told Mom I'd watch the boys tonight while she's making Mexican wedding cakes."

"Who's getting married?" asked Amy as she pulled on her parka.

"No one," said Carlie. "They're actually just cookies, but Mom likes to make them for holidays."

"I'll clean up," said Morgan as she picked up the paper plates and napkins and tossed them into a bag.

"Thanks!" called Carlie and Amy in unison. "See ya."

Morgan took her time cleaning up the bus. She put all the garbage away, then put the leftover sodas in the fridge and the chips in the cupboard. She wiped down the table and the counter and sink. Then she even went around and fluffed the pillows and things before she finally unplugged the strings of lights and turned off the heater. "Good-bye, old faithful bus," she said as she turned off the last light. "Happy Thanksgiving."

Back at her house, Morgan retreated to her bedroom. She knew that her mom was going out tonight with some single girlfriends who got together occasionally. She also knew that since it was Wednesday, Grandma would expect her to go to midweek service with her. The problem was that Morgan did not feel like going. She knew she should probably go anyway. Pastor George often said that the best time to go to church was when you felt the least like going, but somehow she didn't think she could force herself tonight.

Morgan's plan was to lie low. She would keep the light off in her room and pretend to be napping. Maybe Grandma would lose track of the time and forget all about going to church. After all, she was pretty wrapped up with getting things ready for tomorrow's Thanksgiving feast. Because, as it turned out, Emily's family and Mr. Greeley were still coming over. Just another reminder for Morgan that her best friend was off having fun with someone else.

At quarter past seven, it was late enough that Morgan knew they wouldn't be going to church. But now she felt a little concerned too — as well as hungry. Grandma would usually have called Morgan to dinner by now. Maybe she actually went to church without her. Morgan went out into the living room and looked around. No Grandma. The kitchen was dark too. Then Morgan checked out the kitchen window, peeking into the carport, but Grandma's car was there. Was it possible that Grandma had gone out with someone else tonight? Morgan looked around to see if there was a note. No note.

Finally Morgan decided to peek into Grandma's room, although it seemed unlikely that she'd be in here. And there, with only a bedside lamp on, Grandma was stretched out on top of her bed with her Bible still open in her lap. Morgan felt a jolt of panic, like something was seriously wrong — was Grandma dead? Then she walked closer and saw that Grandma was breathing. She was simply asleep. Morgan tiptoed out of the bedroom and went to the kitchen to find something to eat. It looked like Grandma had been busy today. Lots of things, including several yummy-looking pies, were all ready to go for tomorrow. A big turkey occupied most of the refrigerator. No wonder Grandma was so tired.

Morgan fixed herself a peanut butter sandwich and a glass of milk, which she took to the living room to eat in front of the TV. Normally, this wasn't allowed, but since Mom was gone and Grandma was asleep, who would know? She turned on the TV, going to the Disney channel, but the show playing, of course, was about a ski trip. Morgan turned off the TV and ate her sandwich in silence. All she could think was that, right now, Emily was with Chelsea, having the time of her life. She was enjoying a fancy dinner in a ski lodge, complete with live music — how could Morgan ever compete with something like that?

"What are you doing, Morgan?" asked Grandma as she came out of her bedroom.

"Oh …" Morgan looked up with a guilty expression. "I was all alone and hungry … and I just thought —"

"I'm sorry," said Grandma as she looked at the clock on the wall. "I had no idea it was so late. I thought I'd take a little rest. Goodness, what happened to the time?"

"It looks like you were busy today," said Morgan as she polished off the last of her milk. "Sorry I wasn't around to help."

"Oh, that's all right."

Morgan followed Grandma into the kitchen. But it seemed like Grandma was moving slower than usual. "Are you okay?" Morgan asked her.

Grandma turned and looked at her. "Well, yes ... just tired, I guess ..." She smiled. "Getting old."

"Anything I can help you with?" offered Morgan.

"Not tonight ... but I might take you up on that tomorrow. Did you get enough to eat, dear?"

"Yeah, I'm fine." Then Morgan sat on the kitchen stool and watched as Grandma put a bowl of soup into the microwave.

"Are you still feeling badly about Emily not being here for Thanksgiving?"

Morgan shrugged. "I'm okay." She'd already confessed some of her sadness to Grandma, but now she wanted to pretend like it wasn't such a big deal.

"Have you tried out the sock pattern with the tiger stripes yet?" Grandma sat down on the stool opposite Morgan and dipped her spoon into the soup she'd just heated. "I found some other nice remnants of polar fleece the other day. I think there might be enough for several pairs of socks."

"I haven't tried the pattern yet," admitted Morgan. "I'd been hoping that Emily and I could work on it tomorrow and into the weekend ... but that's not going to happen."

"Maybe you and I could work on it together," offered Grandma.

"Sure," said Morgan. And she knew it was nice of Grandma to want to help and she didn't want to hurt her feelings, but it just wouldn't be the same as having Emily here.

The next morning, Morgan did what she could to help Grandma in the kitchen. But with Mom home, it seemed more like Morgan was in the way. And then when Mr. Greeley and Emily's family came, all Morgan could think was that it wasn't fair that Emily wasn't here. She tried to be polite during dinner, but all she wanted to do was to get away from these people. It was all wrong. Finally, as everyone was taking a break before dessert, Morgan excused herself.

"I think I'll take a walk," she said.

"Right now?" said Mom with a creased brow. "It's raining like the dickens out there."

"I'll wear my rain slicker." And then Morgan made a quick exit. But Mom was right; it was really coming down hard. Soon Morgan found herself unlocking the door to the clubhouse. She turned on the heater and the string of lights and proceeded to make herself at home. She tried not to think about what Emily and Chelsea were doing right now. But it was like telling herself not to think about pink elephants — the more she tried to push it from her mind, the more obsessed she became. Since it was raining down here, it was probably snowing up there. Snow sure seemed a lot nicer than rain. She wondered if Emily was wearing Chelsea's Tommy Hilfiger outfit. Were they having a great time riding down the mountain together? Was Emily as good as Chelsea? Or maybe she was better. Morgan remembered Emily's promise to give Morgan lessons on Kyle's skateboard, but that hadn't happened yet. Finally, Morgan was sick and tired of thinking about Emily and Chelsea. Maybe being stuck at home with her family and Emily's and even Mr. Greeley would be better than this!

Besides, Morgan told herself as she jogged back through the rain, she could start making polar socks. If she set her mind to it, she might even have several pairs finished by the end of the day. She wondered how many pairs it would take to make fifty dollars — five pairs if she charged ten for each pair, but that seemed a little steep.

"You're back," said Mom as Morgan burst in out of the rain.

"Yeah, it's pretty wet out there."

"Well, Mr. Greeley and Lisa and Kyle just left."

"Did they already have dessert?"

"Yes, and everyone was starting to act sleepy. I think they all went home to take a nap."

"That sounds good to me," said Grandma.

"Yes," said Mom. "You go and have a rest. Morgan and I will clean up in here."

Morgan wanted to protest this idea, but knew that would be selfish ... especially since she hadn't helped much to get things ready. So she rolled up her sleeves and helped Mom to put the kitchen back in order.

"Grandma said that you were missing Emily," said Mom as she handed Morgan a pan to dry.

Morgan just shrugged. "I guess ..."

"Lisa said that Emily had been so thrilled to go, Morgan. You know life hasn't been exactly easy for them this past year. Emily has been through a lot. Really, you should be happy for her."

Morgan forced a smile. "Okay, I am happy for her. I guess I'm just sad for me."

Mom laughed and gave Morgan a little hug. "Well, at least that's honest."

"And I'm worried," confessed Morgan.

"About what?"

"Well, what if Emily and Chelsea become best friends?"

"I suppose that could happen ..." Mom handed Morgan a pie tin to dry. "At least you have several good friends, Morgan. There's Carlie and Amy still."

"I know ... but Emily is my best friend."

"Then my guess is that she will continue to be your best friend."

"I hope so."

"Morgan ..." Mom had a slightly worried expression now.

"What?"

"Well, I'm concerned about your grandma."

"Why?"

"She hasn't been feeling well lately. She's very tired and ... and it seems like she's just not herself."

"What's wrong?"

"I don't know. I'm encouraging her to see the doctor, but she thinks it's just old age."

"How old is Grandma anyway?"

"Not that old. She's not even seventy yet."

"Oh." Morgan didn't want to admit it, but that seemed pretty old.

"Anyway, until we can get her to go to the doctor, I want both of us to help out more around here. Are you okay with that?"

"Of course."

"Maybe we can take turns fixing dinner," said Mom.

Morgan made a face. "But we're not as good at cooking as Grandma."

"I know. But that might be because we never get the chance to practice."

"But Grandma loves to cook."

"Well, we can help with other things too. You're old enough to do your own laundry. And I can start doing some of the grocery shopping."

Morgan studied Mom for a moment. "Do you really think she's sick?"

Mom just shook her head. "I don't know."

So when Morgan went to bed on Thanksgiving night, she had two things to worry about — losing her best friend, and her grandmother's health. But instead of worrying, Morgan did something better. She prayed.

chapter five

When Morgan got up on the day after Thanksgiving, she discovered Grandma sitting at the kitchen table with her sewing basket and a small pile of colorful polar fleece. "Good morning," said Grandma brightly.

"Good morning." Morgan eyed the fleece. "Is that for making socks?"

"Yes. I thought you and I could work on it together. Your mom already went to open up her shop early. You know what they say about today."

"Black Friday?" asked Morgan.

Grandma chuckled. "Yes, the biggest shopping day of the year."

"I wish I had thought about that sooner," said Morgan. "I could've had some socks all made up to sell in Mom's shop today."

"Oh, well," said Grandma. "No use crying over spilt milk."

"Did you have breakfast already?" asked Morgan.

Grandma smiled sheepishly. "Well, I wasn't very hungry after all that feasting yesterday. I had pumpkin pie and coffee. Are you hungry?" Grandma started to get up.

"No," said Morgan quickly. "I just want cold cereal. I can get it."

Grandma held up the paper pattern. "I've been reading the instructions. I see that we use this pattern as a model to create several other patterns in various sizes."

"Oh, yeah," said Morgan as she filled a bowl with Cheer-ios. "I never even thought about sizes."

"Apparently somebody else did. While you're up, do you want to get me that roll of butcher paper out of the drawer?"

Morgan found the paper and handed it to Grandma, then sat down across from her and began eating cereal.

"I'll just trace these out on the paper," said Grandma as she adjusted her glasses. "You can cut them."

By noon they had all the patterns cut, and Morgan was just getting ready to cut out the fabric when Grandma seemed to grow weary. "Why don't you go have a rest," said Morgan. "I can work on these."

"I do feel tired," said Grandma.

Morgan stood up now. "Come on," she urged as she helped Grandma up. "You have a little nap and then you can help me later, okay?"

"You and Cleo," said Grandma. "You're treating me like an old lady."

"Because we love you," said Morgan.

Grandma laughed as she walked, but Morgan also noticed that she put her hand on the counter to balance herself. That was not like her.

"Come on, Grandma," said Morgan as she took her by the arm. "Let me walk with you."

"I do feel a little unsteady sometimes," admitted Grandma. "A little light-headed when I stand up."

"Mom said you need to go to the doctor," said Morgan as she walked her to her bedroom.

"Oh, I don't know about—"

"And while you're resting, I'm going to call Dr. Ballister and make an appointment for you."

"Oh, you are, are you?" Grandma peered at Morgan.

"Isn't that what you would do for me if I was feeling sick?"

Grandma chuckled as Morgan helped her to her bed. "You're growing up too fast, Morgan. It seems like only yesterday that I was putting you down for a nap ... now you're doing the same to me."

Morgan laid Grandma's crocheted afghan over her legs. "Just rest, Grandma. I'll see if I can get you an appointment for next week. Okay?"

"Whatever you say, dear."

So Morgan closed the door behind her and went out and looked up Dr. Ballister's phone number. She explained the concerns they had about Grandma as well as the symptoms of tiredness and dizziness and the nurse made an appointment for the following Tuesday. Morgan wrote down the time and date, thanked her, and hung up.

Morgan returned to the kitchen, and instead of going back to her sewing project, she cleaned up the breakfast dishes, washed out the coffee pot, and then went back to cutting out socks. She realized right away that it would be important to pin the pieces together so that the sizes didn't get mixed up. She also made some mistakes with cutting the fabric with the wrong side out. But finally, she had what appeared to be eight pairs of socks, in various sizes, ready to sew together. It really didn't seem too complicated.

"How's it going?" asked Grandma as Morgan was setting up her sewing machine.

"You're up from your nap," said Morgan. "Feeling better?"

"I can hardly believe I slept so long. Do you know that it's after one already?"

Morgan showed her how many pairs of socks she cut out. "I was just about to sew up this first pair. They're my size, so I thought I could test them out to make sure I'm doing it right."

"Good thinking. And don't forget to use the knit stitch. It takes longer, but it's the only way you can sew a stretchy fabric like that fleece without having the seams pop open."

"I know," said Morgan. "I just wish it wasn't such a slow way to sew."

"Better slowly than holey."

Morgan laughed as she changed the stitch setting. "Some people might like 'holy' socks."

"Not ones with holes in them. And while you're doing that, I'll go put us together some lunch. We have some fine-looking turkey leftovers."

"Sounds yummy."

By the time Grandma called her to lunch, Morgan had one sock completely finished in the tiger design. She proudly took it in to show Grandma.

"It looks fine, Morgan. Did it fit okay?"

"I haven't tried it yet." Morgan sat down in a chair in the living room and peeled off her shoe and sock. "I guess it doesn't matter which foot I put it on, does it?"

"Not for socks, dear."

"Ugh," groaned Morgan as she tried to force her foot into the sock. "This is not working . . . not at all."

"Let me see," said Grandma.

Morgan handed her the sock. "It doesn't stretch, you know, to go over my foot. It's too tight."

Grandma examined the sock and finally nodded. "I see what's wrong."

"What?"

Grandma stretched the fabric. "See?"

"What?"

"The stretch is going the wrong way. You need to cut them out so that the stretch goes widthwise. This one goes lengthwise. That's why you couldn't get your foot into it."

"Oh no," said Morgan. "I never thought about that when I cut out the other socks. What if they're all wrong?"

"I doubt that they'll all be wrong, dear."

"But some of them will be."

"At least it was only remnant fabric," said Grandma. "Come and have some lunch, and we'll figure it out later."

"I can't believe I was so stupid," said Morgan as she sat down at the kitchen table. "You've told me about the grain of the fabric before."

After lunch, they went to Morgan's room to see what could be done about the sock dilemma. Morgan held up a pair of cut-out socks that were neatly pinned together. "I thought I was being so careful," she said, "and all I did was mess things up."

"Don't be so hard on yourself. I probably would've done the same thing. I've knit socks before, but making them out of fabric is new to me too." Grandma sat on Morgan's bed and examined the pieces that she had cut out, separating into two piles the ones that were going the right way from the ones that were going the wrong way. But the wrong-way pile was getting bigger and bigger.

"This is hopeless," said Morgan as she flopped down into her beanbag chair.

Grandma chuckled. "Well, it looks like you have two pairs that are cut in the right direction."

"All that work for just two pairs of socks," said Morgan sadly. "And I haven't even sewn them yet."

"Just consider it a learning experience."

"But what about all the fabric I wasted?" Morgan looked at the big pile of colorful pieces.

Grandma smiled. "Well, don't throw these away. I think I might be able to piece them together for a quilt."

"A sock quilt?"

Grandma laughed. "Maybe so … maybe so …"

"I guess I should be glad that Emily isn't here."

"Why's that, dear?"

"Because she'd probably think I was an idiot to waste all this time and fabric to produce just two pairs of socks."

"You haven't even produced those yet," Grandma reminded her. "Why don't you sew them up and see how it goes. Then maybe we can make a trip to the fabric store and get some more polar fleece fabric. They're having a big sale today."

"You want to go shopping on Black Friday?"

Grandma patted her on the head. "If it'll help get you out of these doldrums, I do." Then she winked at Morgan. "Besides, you know me, I'm always happy to go to the fabric store."

So Morgan sewed up the socks and was surprised that it didn't take as long as she thought it would. She even tried a pair on — the ones with red and white stripes — and they fit perfectly. She proudly modeled them for Grandma.

"How do they feel?"

"Great. I think I'll keep them." Then Morgan looked at the other pair. They were soft pastel colors. "Hey, these are your size, Grandma. Why don't you try them on?"

"Oh, I don't want to —"

"Come on," said Morgan. "Just try them."

So Grandma slipped off her slippers and pulled on the fuzzy socks. "Very nice," she said, pointing a toe.

"They're for you," proclaimed Morgan.

"Thank you very much."

Then Grandma and Morgan went to the fabric store. Morgan only had twelve dollars of her own money, but Grandma offered to help out. "Look at all these colors," said Morgan as they walked down the aisle of polar fleece fabric. "I don't know how I'll decide." But before long, Morgan had picked out a stack of bolts. Grandma helped her to figure out the yardage, and according to their esti-mates, Morgan would be able to make about thirty pairs of socks when she was all done. "That's if I don't cut them wrong," said Morgan as they went out to the car.

"I think today's lesson will take care of that."

"Thanks for your help, Grandma," said Morgan as she opened the bag and fingered the soft fabric. "Do you think eight dollars a pair is too much?"

"I think that sounds about right for handmade socks," said Grandma. "I know my feet are nice and cozy right now. And these socks are just perfect for my rain boots."

By Saturday afternoon, Morgan had sewn up three pairs of socks. She was just about to start another pair when Grandma called her to come out of her room. "Amy is here to see you," she said.

"Oh, hi, Amy," said Morgan, wondering why Amy had on a dress. "What's up?"

"Miss McPhearson's tea," said Amy in a slightly irritated tone. "And you do not look ready to go."

Morgan slapped her forehead. "Oh, man, I totally forgot." She looked at the clock on the wall. "Do I have time to change real quick?"

"Just hurry," commanded Amy. "Carlie is in the car. My sister An is driving us over there."

Morgan rushed back to her room, opened her closet, and pulled out a dark green velvet jumper that Grandma made for her last Christmas. She didn't really like the jumper because she felt it looked too juvenile. But she figured Miss McPhearson might appreciate it. And it would make Grandma happy. Hopefully it wasn't too small. She tugged it over her white turtleneck, and fortunately it fit. Then she shoved her feet into her black knee-high boots and added a beaded necklace. She grabbed up her coat and was about to hurry out when she noticed a finished pair of purple socks on her bed. Would it be too weird to give them to Miss McPhearson? She stuffed them into her coat pocket, and then hurried back to the living room. She could figure that out later.

"Wow, that was quick," said Amy, peering curiously at Morgan's outfit as she pulled on her coat.

"Don't you look pretty," said Grandma. "You girls have fun now."

Morgan thought that was probably unlikely. She did like Miss McPhearson, but the old woman could be moody sometimes. And it would probably set her off if her young guests arrived late. But fortunately, they made it on time. Cara, Miss McPhearson's housekeeper and Amy's friend, answered the door and took them to the parlor. "May I take your coats?" she asked. As the other girls gave her their coats, Morgan slipped the purple socks from her pocket and rolled them up and hid them in her hand. Maybe it was silly to give Miss McPhearson socks. She didn't even know if they would fit. But it was too late to put them back in her coat pocket because Cara was taking their coats away.

"Welcome," said Miss McPhearson as she entered the room. "Please, have a seat."

The three girls sat down and, as usual, Miss McPhearson directed most of her conversation to Amy. Amy was the one who originally befriended the lonely old woman.

But the other girls had gotten to know her as well. And as odd as it might seem to someone who didn't get it, they all got along fairly well. At least as long as the girls minded their manners. Miss McPhearson was a stickler for manners. Sometimes Morgan thought the purpose of their visits and teas was so that she could turn them all into little ladies. Still, it was interesting, and Miss McPhearson's house, set high on a bluff overlooking the ocean, was like a museum full of interesting old stories.

"What's that in your hand, Morgan?" Miss McPhearson asked as Amy poured the tea.

Morgan swallowed. "I, uh, I brought something for you, Miss McPhearson."

"Well, what is it?" the old woman said impatiently.

"Something I made," explained Morgan. "But I'm not sure they're the right size. I wasn't really thinking."

Miss McPhearson held out her hand, and Morgan set the pair of socks in it. "What is this?"

"They're socks," said Morgan. "Polar fleece socks. I made some for my grandma, and she really liked them. I thought you might like them too."

Miss McPhearson unrolled the socks and held them out to examine them. "Very interesting, Morgan. Thank you very much."

"You're welcome."

Then Miss McPhearson set the bright purple socks aside in a way that made Morgan think it had probably been a mistake after all. "Where are the other girls?" she asked. "Emily and Chelsea?" Amy explained about the ski trip, and Miss McPhearson immediately launched into a colorful story about the first time she and her family went skiing, up at the very same lodge, and how she broke her leg on the very first run. "I never skied again."

Morgan just hoped that wouldn't be the case with Emily. Or Chelsea, for that matter. She shot up a little prayer for both of them to come home safely and in one piece.

chapter six

Morgan missed Emily at church on Sunday. And although she sat with Mom and Grandma, she felt lonely. It seemed wrong not having Emily there, not sitting up in the front pew together. And it didn't feel right having a whole Sunday afternoon without Emily, and without having a meeting at the clubhouse since Amy was working and Carlie was watching her brothers. But Morgan used the afternoon to sew up more socks. By the time Mom told her to go to bed, she had ten pairs completely finished.

"Can you sell these in your store?" Morgan asked her mom.

Mom examined a pair of red and green socks. "I don't see why not. Can you think of a way to connect them together so the pairs don't get mixed up? Maybe make a tag with the size and the price on it?"

"Sure."

The next morning, Morgan got up early and made tags for her socks. She sewed a piece of yarn to connect the socks and the tags. Then she emptied her scarf basket and filled it with the ten pairs of socks. By the time she finished, she thought the whole thing looked very professional.

"Here you go, Mom," she said as she handed over the basket.

"I'll put it by the cash register," Mom promised. "People seem to notice things up there."

"Do you think eight dollars a pair is too much?"

Mom considered this. "I guess we'll find out."

Morgan hurried to finish her breakfast and then gathered up her things for school and was just going out the door when Grandma asked why she was going so early.

"I just wanted some extra time to see Emily," said Morgan. "I want to hear about the ski trip without having everyone else around."

Grandma smiled. "Oh, yes. I see."

It was drizzling outside, so Morgan pulled on her hood and jogged over to Emily's house, knocking loudly on the door.

"Oh, hi, Morgan," said Mrs. Adams. "Emily's not here."

Morgan frowned. "Where is she? Did she get hurt snowboarding?"

Mrs. Adams laughed. "No, but they got home so late last night, Emily spent the night at Chelsea's."

"Oh."

"Sorry. But you'll see her at school."

"Yeah…"

Morgan trudged back home.

"What's wrong?" asked Grandma when Morgan went back into the house and dumped her backpack by the front door.

"Nothing…" Morgan stood near the door, just staring at her somewhat soggy reflection in the hallway mirror. Her glasses were splattered with rain, and her beaded braids looked droopier than usual.

Grandma came over and stood behind her. "Is something wrong with Emily? Is she sick or hurt?"

"She spent the night at Chelsea's," said Morgan sadly.

"Oh." Grandma nodded as she fingered one of Morgan's beaded braids. "And you're feeling bad?"

"I guess…" Morgan turned and looked at Grandma. "Do you think I should lose the braids?"

"What?" Grandma blinked.

"My beaded braids. I was thinking maybe I'm too old for them now."

Grandma smiled. "Well, I think that's up to you, dear."

"I think I want to have normal hair now. You know, like my friends."

Grandma nodded. "Well, I'm sure that can be arranged."

"Maybe I can use some of my sock money to do that," said Morgan eagerly. "I mean I don't know how much it'll cost … but I think it will be worth it." Then she pointed to her glasses. "And maybe I should get contacts too."

Grandma frowned. "Why are you so interested in changing yourself, Morgan?"

"I don't know."

"Is it because you're worried about Emily?" asked Grandma. "You think she might like Chelsea more than she likes you? You think that changing yourself will make a difference?"

Morgan shrugged. "I think I'm just tired of looking like this all the time. I think it's time for a change."

"Well, as long as you're doing it for the right reasons …"

"Doing what for the right reasons?" asked Mom as she came out of her bedroom dressed for work.

So Morgan explained her idea for changing her hair and getting contacts. Mom blinked in surprise. "Wow, that's a lot to change all at once. And getting your curls relaxed and getting contacts won't be cheap."

Morgan pointed to her sock basket. "But I could use some of my sock money. And I could buy more fabric and make more socks."

Mom grinned. "You certainly are industrious."

"So, do you think I could do that?"

"Is that what you really want?" asked Mom.

Morgan nodded eagerly. "Yeah, I do."

"Well, let me give Crystal a call and see if she can get you scheduled for hair. As far as the contacts go, why don't you give that a little more thought, Morgan?"

So Morgan agreed. Then, since it was raining even harder now, Mom offered to give her and her friends a lift to school. And as Morgan rode in the front, with Carlie and Amy in the back, she imagined how she would look with her new hair. Her plan was to keep her mini makeover a complete secret. Even from Emily. She would surprise everyone.

"There's Chelsea's car," said Carlie as Mom pulled up in front of the school. And soon all five friends were clustered together in front of their lockers. Chelsea and Emily were telling the others about the spectacular time they had riding the slopes, and how they even met some cute boys who thought they were in high school, and how they'd both gotten really good at snowboarding.

"We had a nice time at Miss McPhearson's on Saturday," said Amy, as if that could compete with Chelsea and Emily's weekend. Then the warning bell was ringing, and they all headed off to their first class.

"I can't wait until the ski trip," Emily told Morgan on their way to English. "It's going to be totally awesome."

"I started sewing socks," said Morgan. "It's not very hard, once you figure it out, and I think it'll be a good way to make money for the ski trip."

"I have a plan for making money too," said Emily.

"What's that?"

"Babysitting."

"Babysitting?"

"Yeah, Mrs. Landers has some friends who wanted someone to watch their kids while they go to a Christmas party next Saturday night. I guess it's supposed to last until really late. Mrs. Landers said I could make a lot of money in just one night. She said it might be close to a hundred dollars if the parents tip me. And the kids will mostly be sleeping."

"I didn't know you liked to babysit."

"I used to babysit sometimes … before we moved here."

"Oh."

"Anyway, it's all set," said Emily as they went into English.

"Cool," said Morgan. Although she really thought it stunk. She had hoped that she and Emily could do the sock project together. She had imagined them taking turns cutting and sewing, then selling them together at the bazaar. Now it looked like Emily had a completely different plan. A plan that didn't include Morgan. Still, Morgan knew that she should be happy for her friend. This meant that Emily would for sure be able to do the ski trip. Unless the babysitting thing didn't work out. Making a hundred dollars in one night did sound pretty farfetched. Besides, that was only half of what Emily needed.

Morgan glanced over at Emily, as they sat across from each other in English. It seemed like something had changed about her. Oh, she had the same blonde hair, same blue eyes, same petite frame, but something was different. Then it hit Morgan. Of course, she was wearing Chelsea's clothes. Not only that, but she seemed to be sitting up straighter. Like she had some new sense of confidence. Was it because she was dressed like Chelsea? Or was it something more? Just then, Morgan noticed Mrs. Robertson giving her a warning look, and Morgan knew it was time to pay attention.

Morgan tried to put worrisome thoughts about Emily out of her mind during her morning classes. So what if Emily and Chelsea were friends. Morgan was their friend too. Besides, Morgan still had Amy and Carlie. And they had their clubhouse. Maybe Morgan should plan a meeting for this afternoon.

"We need to try on our elf costumes today," said Chelsea as the five girls sat together for lunch. "That way if we need to alter any of them, there will be time to get it done before Saturday."

"Want to do it at the clubhouse?" suggested Morgan. "I thought maybe we should have a meeting today anyway."

"No," said Chelsea. "I think you should come out to my house this afternoon. There's more room to try stuff on there. Besides, I think my mom wants to see us dressed up. In fact, I'll call her and tell her to order some pizza. And she can give us a ride after school. How's that sound?"

Everyone, except Morgan, thought that was a great plan. And Morgan didn't let on that she wasn't overly thrilled. She wished they could meet at the clubhouse — that things could be the way they had been. But already, Chelsea was letting everyone use her phone to call their parents and make sure it was okay to go home with Chelsea after school.

"Your turn," said Chelsea, handing Morgan the phone.

Morgan dialed her home number and waited for Grandma to answer.

"I'm so glad you called, honey," said Grandma happily. "Your mom called a while ago and it looks like Crystal can get you in for your hair today. I'll pick you up after school and take you over."

"That's great," said Morgan. "See ya then." She hung up and handed the phone back to Chelsea. Then, putting on a disappointed face, she said. "It looks like I can't make it this afternoon."

"Why not?" demanded Chelsea.

"I have an appointment. My grandma has to pick me up right after school."

"But I thought you were going to help us redesign the elf outfits, Morgan," said Chelsea.

"Yeah," said Emily. "You're really good at that."

Morgan considered this. In a way it was both flattering and encouraging. "Well, could we do the fitting tomorrow instead?"

Chelsea frowned. "I guess …"

"I can't," said Carlie. "I promised Mom I'd watch the boys."

"I'm out too," said Amy. "I have to work."

"Well, what if I came over after my appointment?" suggested Morgan. "Although it might be late … like around five or so."

"That's okay with me," said Chelsea. "We can just hang until you get there."

"Maybe we'll even save some pizza for you," teased Emily.

So it was settled. And Morgan thought maybe it was a good plan after all. She could show up with her cool new hair and surprise everyone at once. It was hard to concentrate on school during the afternoon. Morgan kept wondering what her new hair was going to look like. And what would it feel like? And what if something went wrong? Finally, during math, she realized that worrying wasn't doing her one bit of good. So she shot up a quick prayer. It didn't seem like too much to ask. God could help to make sure that her hair turned out okay.

"How are you feeling?" Morgan asked Grandma when she got into the car.

"Oh, so-so …"

"I hope it's not wearing you out to take me to—"

"No, no … driving isn't a problem at all. And Cleo said to just drop you off and you can walk over to the shop when you're done and ride home with your mom."

"No problem."

"Good luck," said Grandma as she pulled in front of Crystal's salon. "I hope it's all that you want it to be."

Morgan crossed her fingers. Then she told Grandma that she'd already prayed about it. Then Grandma waved and drove away. Still, Morgan felt a little uneasy as she walked into the salon.

"Hey, Morgan," said Crystal. "I hear you want a new do."

Morgan nodded as she removed her coat. "Do you think it'll look good?"

Crystal patted Morgan on the back. "You're such a cutie that I think anything would look good on you."

"I don't want to see it," said Morgan as she got into the chair. "Not until you're all done."

"Deal."

chapter seven

Morgan's eyes got big as she looked at her reflection in the mirror. "Is that really me?" she asked, feeling slightly horrified at the balloon of dark brown hair encircling her head. It was such a change after the beaded braids.

"Don't worry," said Crystal, "the curls should continue to relax."

Morgan nodded, but didn't feel convinced.

"Your mom already paid me, so you're free to go." Crystal handed her a bottle of something. "Put some of this on before you go to bed. Not too much. Read the directions."

Morgan stuffed the bottle into her backpack and glanced at her watch. She suddenly remembered her promise to join her friends at Chelsea's house. Now she wasn't so sure. She wished she had a hat to put on, something to flatten out her really big hair. But she thanked Crystal and headed over to Mom's shop.

"Oh, my," said Mom when Morgan walked in. "You look so different, Morgan." She came over to see it close up. "Do you like it?"

Morgan frowned. "I'm not sure. The curl is supposed to relax more."

Mom nodded as she gave Morgan's curls a squeeze. "Yes, that's how mine is after I get it done too."

"Oh, Morgan!" squealed Maureen, the high school girl that Mom had just hired to help out part-time during the holidays. "Look at you, girlfriend."

Morgan rolled her eyes and let out a groan.

"No, it's cute," said Maureen. "I like it."

"Thanks." Morgan turned to Mom. "I'm supposed to go to Chelsea's to try on our costumes for the parade. Can you give me a ride?"

"You're going to be in the parade?" asked Maureen.

"Yeah ... we're going to be elves."

Maureen laughed. "Well, you'll be a cute elf, Morgan. Hope you can keep that hat on with all that hair."

Morgan was silent as Mom drove her up to Chelsea's house.

"You're not sorry you did it, are you?" asked Mom when she pulled into the driveway.

"Kind of ..."

"You'll get used to it, sweetie."

"Yeah, sure ..." Morgan didn't want to talk about her hair, didn't want to think about her hair and, more than anything, she didn't want to show her friends her hair. She wished that she'd never gotten it changed. What had she been thinking? "Thanks for the ride."

"Call me when you're done," said Mom.

"Thanks."

Then, feeling like a lamb being led to the slaughter, Morgan trudged up to Chelsea's front door.

"Morgan?" said Chelsea's mom. "Is that you?"

Morgan nodded. "Yeah, unfortunately."

"Did you change your hair?"

"Don't ask."

Mrs. Landers chuckled. "Well, I suppose it might take some getting used to, but I think it's really pretty, Morgan. Just look at all that curl."

"Yeah," said Morgan. "Just look."

"Morgan!" cried Chelsea from the top of the stairs. "What happened to your hair?"

"Your hair!" screeched Emily. "What have you done?"

Soon all four girls were clustered around her. Staring and touching and expressing their regrets.

"I loved your beaded braids," said Emily. "I can't believe you did this."

"Me neither," said Carlie. "I hate my own curls. Why would you trade your braids for curls?"

"The curls are supposed to relax more," said Morgan.

"Do you like it?" asked Amy.

"Of course not," said Morgan.

"Then why did you do it?" demanded Emily.

"I don't know …" Morgan felt on the verge of tears now.

"It's going to be okay," said Chelsea. "Morgan's probably right, it should relax more. In fact …" Chelsea patted her own red curls. "I might have just the thing for you. Come on, Morgan, let's play beauty shop."

Soon Morgan was seated in front of Chelsea's dressing table. Chelsea was putting something in her hands, rubbing it around and then she was rubbing it into Morgan's hair. She twisted and tugged and rubbed and slowly, slowly, Morgan's hair began to settle down.

"Wow," said Emily. "That's looking really good, Chelsea."

"Yeah, maybe you should become a beautician," said Amy.

"Chelsea's helped me with my hair," said Carlie, putting a hand on both Chelsea's and Morgan's shoulders. "We curly-heads need to stick together."

"Guess we straight-heads should stick together too," said Amy as she put her arm around Emily. Then they all laughed.

"Thanks, Chelsea," said Morgan as she stared at her image in the mirror. "That really is better. Although I wish I had my beaded braids back."

"You'll get used to it," said Chelsea.

"I'm actually starting to like it," said Emily.

Morgan felt a little better. And soon they were all trying on their elf costumes, which really did need some help.

"I don't know about you guys," said Morgan as she looked at herself in Chelsea's full-length mirror. "But I am not going out in public with my rear end showing through these green tights."

"Exactly," said Chelsea.

"The hats and shoes are cute," said Emily.

"But we need shorts or skirts or something," said Morgan. She took off the oversized felt collar and held it at her waist like a skirt. "Something like this would work, if it was a little longer."

Before long, Morgan had taped together some newspapers to make a pattern for a circular skirt. "Tell your mom to buy enough felt to make five of these in red," she instructed Chelsea. "I'm sure the lady at the fabric store can help her. And get, let's see, about ten yards of red ribbon to use around the waist." Then Morgan took the scissors to the huge collars and after a bit of trimming and shaping, they didn't look too bad.

The girls explained their plan to Mrs. Landers and she completely agreed. "Morgan, you really are good at design."

"And Chelsea is really good at hair," said Morgan as she patted her tamed-down curls.

"I'll pick up the fabric tomorrow afternoon," said Mrs. Landers. "Can I drop it by your house after school then, Morgan?"

"Sure," said Morgan. "And maybe we can have a fitting by Thursday."

Soon the girls were downstairs eating pizza, and Morgan kept telling herself that she should be happy. Here she was with her good friends, having a good time ... but something was still bugging her. She couldn't help but notice the connection that seemed to be growing between Chelsea and Emily. They made what seemed like private jokes about things that happened on the slopes. They talked about clothes as if Emily could actually afford to buy them. Finally, just when Morgan felt she couldn't stand it any longer, Mrs. Landers announced that Amy's sister was here to pick her up.

"Anyone need a ride?" offered Amy.

"Sure," said Morgan.

"Me too," said Carlie.

"My mom is picking me up after work," said Emily. "But that's not for an hour. Maybe I should go ahead and ride with — "

"That's okay," said Chelsea. "Stay here until your mom comes, Em. I want to show you this snowboarding website my brother just emailed me about. They have some awesome stuff and the graphics are totally amazing."

So Emily stayed and the others left. And as An drove them back to the trailer park, Morgan tried not to feel jealous.

"Hey, you're home," said Mom when Morgan came in. "I thought I was going to pick you up."

Morgan explained about the ride. "And we had pizza, so I'm not really hungry." She looked around the living room. "Where's Grandma?"

"Resting."

"Oh ..."

"I'm so glad you made that doctor's appointment for her," said Mom. "I plan to take her in tomorrow afternoon, and then I'll stick around to hear what's really going on."

Morgan nodded.

Mom patted Morgan's hair. "Hey, it looks better already. I think I'm getting used to it."

"I forgot to ask, Mom, did any socks sell today?"

Mom frowned. "It was pretty quiet in the shop. But then I suppose that's because so many people were out shopping during the weekend. It'll pick up though. Don't worry."

"I guess I should go make some more socks," said Morgan. "The church bazaar is Saturday."

"What about homework?"

"Yeah, yeah," said Morgan. "I'll do that first."

By the time Morgan finished her homework, she only had time to sew up two pairs of socks. At this rate, she wondered how she'd have many pairs to sell at the bazaar. Or if she'd even make enough money to go on the ski trip.

The next morning, as they were walking to school, Carlie invited the girls to go with her and her dad to cut down Christmas trees on Sunday afternoon. "Dad found out that the Christmas tree permits are only to use for your own family. The trees can't be sold or anything."

"Oh." Morgan sighed. "Well, the youth group is still going to a tree farm on Friday afternoon. Anyone who helps cut trees to sell at the bazaar gets to apply the profits toward the ski-trip expense."

"Are you going?" Emily asked Morgan.

"I don't know …" Morgan considered this. "I think it might be a better use of my time to make socks."

"Last night, Mrs. Landers told me that she might have a babysitting job lined up for me on Friday as well as Saturday," said Emily. "So maybe I should pass on the tree thing too."

"I'm going to pay my deposit for the ski trip today," said Amy. "I don't want to take any chances of missing out."

"I need to go in and pay mine too," said Carlie. "My parents signed the form and everything. Maybe we should go together."

"How about you guys?" Amy asked Morgan and Emily.

"Mine is taken care of," said Emily.

"Huh?" Morgan turned and stared at her. "How'd you do that?"

"Actually, Mrs. Landers paid it for me. She said I can pay her back after my babysitting job. Chelsea was worried that I wouldn't get it in on time ..."

"Oh." Morgan frowned.

"Have you paid your deposit, Morgan?" asked Amy.

"Not yet."

"Well, you better get on it." Amy shook her head with disapproval. "I mean it was your idea in the first place."

Morgan mentally calculated how many pairs of socks she'd need to sell to get fifty dollars. Seven would cover it. She wondered how long it would take for seven pairs to sell at her mom's shop. She'd consider asking Mom for a loan, but Mom had already covered her at the hair salon. And Grandma had already helped her with buying fabric. No, Morgan decided, she was on her own now. Still, it was hard not to feel envious of Emily. It seemed unfair that Chelsea's mom had covered for her. Wasn't this ski trip supposed to be about having faith and trusting God to provide? Still, Morgan wasn't even sure how strong her own faith was at the moment. It seemed more impossible than ever right now.

No one was home when Morgan came home from school. Then she remembered that Mom had taken Grandma to the doctor. Morgan prayed that it would go well, and that the doctor would figure out a way to make Grandma feel better. Then Morgan sat down to sew socks.

She was just starting the first pair when she heard knocking at the door.

"Here you go," said Mrs. Landers as she handed a large plastic bag to Morgan. "I got just what you said to get." She laughed. "In fact, I nearly cleaned out the fabric store of their red felt. The ribbon is in there too. And I got some red thread and pins and things just in case." She smiled. "It's so nice of you to help like this."

Morgan nodded and looked down at the bulky bag. "Sure, Mrs. Landers. No problem." But as she closed the front door, she wasn't so sure. How was Morgan supposed to create five elf skirts *and* sew enough socks to pay her way for the ski trip? This just didn't seem fair. Normally, at a time like this, she might ask Grandma to help. But if Grandma was still feeling tired ... well, maybe that wasn't such a good idea.

Morgan took the pile of red felt and spread out the fabric all over the beige living room carpet. One good thing was that she could use the whole room without worrying about getting in anyone's way. Then she took out her circular newspaper pattern and laid it out and began cutting. At least it was a very simple design. And being that it was felt fabric, it wouldn't involve much sewing. By five o'clock she had all five skirts cut out and ready for their ribbon waistbands to be attached. The only problem was that little pieces of red felt were all over the rug. She didn't want Grandma to come home and see the mess. So before she could even begin sewing, she would need to vacuum. But before she could vacuum, she realized she would need to replace the vacuum cleaner bag. And when she attempted to replace the vacuum cleaner bag, she accidentally dropped the full bag on the kitchen floor. Just as she was attempting to clean up this mess the phone rang.

"Morgan," said Mom. "We're running late. The doctor sent us over to the hospital for some special tests for Grandma, and it's taking longer than we expected."

"Oh, that's okay," said Morgan, relieved that she had more time to clean up her mess.

"What I was hoping is … could you start dinner? I know that Grandma is hungry, and she had some hamburger thawed out that she was going to make spaghetti sauce with."

"I don't know how to do that."

"I know. But there's a package of Hamburger Helper that you could put it with."

"I don't know how to do that either."

"It's easy. You just follow the directions. You *can* follow directions, can't you?"

Morgan sensed the impatience in her mother's voice. "Yes."

"And make a little green salad too."

"Okay."

"We should be home after six."

As she hung up the phone, Morgan looked at the messy kitchen floor and then over at the living room rug, scattered with streaks of red and looking as if a wild animal might have been slaughtered on it. And yet she hadn't sewn a single sock yet. It seemed like her chances of making it to the ski trip were getting slimmer and slimmer.

chapter eight

Somehow Morgan managed to clean things up and get dinner started before Mom and Grandma came home.

"You go and rest," Mom told Grandma. "I know you're worn out from all those tests and things."

Grandma didn't argue, and Mom hung up her coat and then came into the kitchen to help Morgan.

"How did the tests go?" asked Morgan as she sliced a tomato for the salad.

"We won't know for a few days."

Morgan considered telling Mom about the frustrating afternoon she'd had, but she could tell that Mom was worried. No sense in making things worse. Together they finished putting dinner together, then Mom fixed up a tray for Grandma, and Morgan took it in to her.

"Oh, that wasn't necessary," said Grandma when she saw Morgan coming in with the tray.

"Hey, we can spoil you if we want to," said Morgan. "You might as well enjoy it while you can. We'll probably find out that you're perfectly fine in a few days, and then you won't get all this pampering."

Grandma chuckled as Morgan set the tray in front of her. "You make a good point." She slowly opened the paper napkin and set it on her lap. "So how is the sock sewing coming?"

"Okay," said Morgan quickly. She knew there was no need to worry Grandma about her sock concerns.

"Your hair looks nice." Grandma nodded her approval.

"Thanks."

Then Grandma bowed her head and said a blessing, adding an extra line of special thanks for her granddaughter and asking God to help Morgan get enough money for the ski trip.

Morgan smiled. "Thanks, Grandma. I'm sure God listens especially closely to your prayers."

"God listens to everyone's prayers, honey."

Then Morgan returned to her sewing projects. She decided to tackle the elf skirts first. Her plan was to get them out of the way so she could focus exclusively on socks, socks, and more socks. But by the time she finished three of the skirts, she remembered she still had math homework to do. And by the time she finished that, it was time for bed.

"Did you sign up for the ski trip yet?" Amy asked Morgan as they walked to school the next morning.

"Not yet," muttered Morgan.

"Well, the office lady at your church told me that it's filling up fast," said Amy. "You better get on it."

"Yeah," agreed Carlie. "That's what she told me too."

"I will," said Morgan. "I need to see how many pairs of socks have been sold at my mom's shop. Things were so busy last night that I forgot to ask."

"Are you going to church tonight?" asked Emily.

"Is it Wednesday already?" asked Morgan.

"Yeah," said Emily. "And since I missed church last week, I'd really like to go."

"I'll let you know," said Morgan. "My grandma hasn't been feeling too great. It'll probably depend on her." Morgan had actually been hoping that they wouldn't be going tonight, just so she could stay home and finish up her sewing projects. She knew that was probably wrong, but it was the truth.

"How are the elf skirts coming?" asked Carlie.

"Almost done," said Morgan.

"Good," said Amy. "Remember we're supposed to try them on tomorrow."

"Oh, yeah," said Emily, "I just remembered something, Morgan. The youth group was getting together before church tonight —"

"The wreath-making party!" exclaimed Morgan. "I totally forgot."

"Me too," said Emily.

"That sounds like fun," said Carlie. "Can anyone come?"

"Of course," said Morgan. "The reason for making the wreaths is to earn money for the ski trip — they'll divide up the profits from the bazaar with whoever helps out."

"Hey, maybe I can come too," said Amy.

By the time the girls got to school, it was all worked out. Emily's mom had the day off, so she could probably give them a ride to the church. "Just meet at my house a little before four," Emily told them.

But when four o'clock came later that afternoon, Morgan was still sitting at her sewing machine, finishing up the last elf skirt. And when that was done, she started in on socks. She was just finishing up her third pair of socks when Mom called her to dinner. And after dinner, which Mom had cooked, Grandma announced that she wanted to go to church that night.

"You're sure you're up to it?" asked Morgan.

"I think it might energize me," said Grandma as she put on her coat.

"Sounds like just the ticket," said Mom.

As Mom drove them to church, Morgan tried not to obsess over the fact that she was way behind on her sock-sewing project. She knew that all she could do was to trust God. If he wanted her to go on the ski trip, he would have to make it happen.

"There are only three spaces left on the ski trip," Emily told Morgan when they met in the foyer of church. "And there were a couple of kids at the wreath-making party who hadn't even signed up yet."

Morgan shrugged. "Nothing I can do about that."

"But what if you don't get to go?" asked Emily.

She shrugged again.

"You should've come to the wreath-making party," said Emily. "It was really fun. Carlie and Amy got to know some of the kids in youth group, and it was pretty cool. And we made a ton of wreaths. If they all sell at the bazaar, there'll be lots of money for the ski trip."

"Good." Morgan forced a smile to her lips.

They were in the sanctuary now. "Do you want to sit in front?" Emily asked hopefully.

"I guess …" Then Morgan followed Emily up to their favorite spot right in front of Pastor George's podium. But even as she sat down, she felt none of her usual enthusiasm. And as they worshiped, she didn't feel that old thrill. And that spark that normally ignited inside of her felt as if it was barely flickering at all. She knew that wasn't good. But she wasn't sure what to do about it. Finally, she did the only thing she knew — she silently prayed, telling God what was wrong, and then she asked him to help her.

"Are you going to work at the bazaar on Saturday?" Janna asked Morgan after church. "I don't have you down on the schedule yet."

"And we missed you at the wreath-making party," said Cory. "Where you been hiding, Morgan?"

"I had to do some things at home," she told him.

"Well, we have Emily down," said Janna as she looked at the clipboard. "She'll be working from ten to twelve so she can make it to the parade at one. You could work with her if you want." She winked at Morgan. "I'm guessing you'll have all sorts of cool things to sell."

"Yeah," said Emily. "She's making socks."

"Socks?" Janna blinked. "What kind of socks?"

"Polar fleece socks," said Morgan.

"Cool," said Janna. "I might be interested in some of those myself." She jabbed her husband with her elbow. "Cory might want some too. His tootsies can get awfully cold in the winter."

So Morgan felt a little encouraged as they rode home. Maybe her socks would be a success after all. That is if she ever got enough time to sew them all. She knew that tomorrow afternoon was for trying on their elf outfits again — at least the skirts were finished now. Maybe her best bet would be to kick in the afterburners on Friday. She could stay up as late as she liked since it wasn't a school night. She considered asking Emily to help her with the sewing and cutting, maybe even to spend the night, but then she remembered Emily's babysitting gig on that same night.

"How many pairs of socks have sold at your store?" Morgan asked Mom as they went into the house.

"I forgot to check," Mom admitted. "But Maureen said it's been slow."

"Oh…"

"Things should pick up this weekend. What with the Christmas parade, as well as people counting down the shopping days until Christmas."

"And there's the bazaar," Grandma reminded her. "You do plan to sell socks there, don't you?"

"Yeah," said Morgan. She just hoped she'd have some socks to sell. She was tempted to get the ones from Mom's shop, but then she would miss out on the traffic in town. She was also tempted to stay up past her bedtime to sew, but she knew that Mom would not approve. Besides, she was tired. And she was tired of sewing too!

The next day, Chelsea's mom picked up all five girls after school. They went to Chelsea's again to try on the outfits, along with the skirts.

"You did a wonderful job on these skirts," Mrs. Landers, told Morgan as the girls lined up on the stairway, posing for a photo. "You girls will be the cutest thing in the whole parade. Now let's get you by the Christmas tree." The Landers' Christmas tree was huge, reaching up to the peak of their high ceilings. Morgan couldn't imagine how they'd gotten it into the house. It reminded her that her family didn't have a Christmas tree yet. Usually, Grandma took care of that, but with her feeling so rundown these days … maybe Morgan should take up Carlie's offer to go into the woods with her dad to get a tree on Sunday.

"All right," said Mrs. Landers, "You girls know where the staging area for the parade will be. And you need to be there by 12:30. Hopefully it won't rain, but just in case, you might want to dress warmly underneath the costumes. We don't want anyone getting hypothermia."

"Looks like we'll have to wear our elf outfits to work at the bazaar, Morgan," said Emily.

"Maybe that'll help to sell things," said Amy.

"Now if anyone needs a ride," said Mrs. Landers, "I'm going back to town in about fifteen minutes."

"Not that you all have to leave yet," said Chelsea. "Anyone who wants to hang here is welcome."

"I have to get to the restaurant," said Amy.

"And I'm babysitting again," said Carlie.

"I'll stick around," said Emily. "How about you, Morgan, why don't you stay too?"

"I need to go home and sew socks," said Morgan.

"You *sew* socks?" asked Mrs. Landers.

"They're polar fleece socks," Emily explained.

"Oh, what a good idea," said Mrs. Landers. "I might like some of those for myself."

"My mom has some at her shop," offered Morgan hopefully.

"Cleopatra's, right?"

"Yes," said Morgan. "Eight dollars a pair."

"I'll make a point to stop by this weekend."

Morgan felt hopeful as Mrs. Landers drove the girls home. Still, she felt slightly jealous that Emily stayed behind. It was nice of Emily to invite Morgan to stay too, but it would've been nicer if Emily had come home with them and maybe even helped Morgan with her sock project. Still, Morgan hadn't asked Emily. And why would Emily want to help Morgan when she could stay at Chelsea's and just hang and have fun?

Morgan thanked Mrs. Landers for the ride, told Amy and Carlie good-bye, and then went into her house. As usual, Grandma had *Oprah* on, but she was fast asleep in her recliner. Morgan tiptoed past her and went straight to her room and her sewing machine. Her goal was to get four pairs of socks finished before dinnertime. And then she had a pile of homework to do. She had barely started the second pair of socks when she heard a tapping on her door. "Come in," she called without looking up from her sewing machine.

"Morgan," said Mom in a quiet voice. "I need to talk to you."

Morgan glanced at the clock by her bed. It wasn't even five yet. "You're home early," she told Mom as she turned around in her chair.

Mom sat on her bed. "It's about Grandma."

"What?"

"We got the test results back."

Morgan frowned. "Is it bad?"

"Grandma has some very serious problems with her heart."

"Oh no …" Morgan felt a lump growing in her throat. "What does that mean?"

"It means that unless she has surgery … well, she could have a heart attack … and it could be fatal."

"So, is she going to have the surgery?"

"Yes. Of course. But in the meantime, she needs to really take it easy. You and I will have to do everything around here. I know you've been helping already, but with Christmas coming … well, you know how Grandma loves this time of year. She gets so busy with her baking and crafts and decorating and everything. But we cannot let her do that."

"Right."

"If it was up to me, I'd say we just cancel Christmas altogether this year." Mom scowled. "I know I sound like Scrooge."

"We can't cancel Christmas."

"I know … and Grandma would be so sad if we did. No, we need to try to do as much as we can of the things that she usually does. She's already mentioned the fact that we haven't put up lights yet."

"I'll do that," said Morgan.

"And she wants a tree."

"I can go with Carlie and her dad on Sunday and get one in the woods for only five dollars."

Mom blinked. "Really, you can get a tree for five dollars?"

"With a permit."

"Great." Mom actually smiled now. "I'm so thankful we're in this together, Morgan."

"When will Grandma have the surgery?"

"Next week. They're trying to get her scheduled now."

"Is the surgery dangerous?"

"All surgery is a little dangerous, Morgan."

"But she'll be okay?"

"Yes, I'm sure she will." Mom looked at the pile of un-sewn socks. "How's the sock-sewing business coming?"

"Slow."

"Oh, I did check on your socks. It looks like five pairs have sold."

Morgan frowned. "That's all?"

"I thought that was pretty good considering how slow it's been."

"But that's not even enough to pay for my deposit on the ski trip."

Mom stood up and ran her fingers through Morgan's curls. "Well, here's the good news: I'm not going to make you pay me back for getting your hair done."

Morgan brightened. "Thanks, Mom."

"And I'll go ahead and pay you for the socks you've sold. That's forty dollars. And I'll advance you the other ten. I'm sure we'll sell more socks this weekend. In fact, I'm hoping you'll have some more ready for me soon. Your basket was looking empty."

"I'll bring you everything that's leftover from the bazaar."

"Great. I'm going to start dinner now."

"How about if I put up the Christmas lights?"

"That would be fantastic. The lights and decorations are in those red and green storage bins out in the storage shed. You might as well bring all of them to the back porch so we can start going through them."

So Morgan set aside her sewing, put on her coat, and went out to the shed. At least she had her deposit money now. That was something.

chapter nine

On Friday, Morgan's plan was to go straight home from school. She tried not to feel bad when Emily said she was riding home with Chelsea. She knew it was because Emily was going to be babysitting for friends of the Landers. It was business. Still, it was hard not to be just a little bit jealous.

"I'd like to go with you and your dad to get a tree on Sunday," Morgan told Carlie as they walked together. Amy had already turned off toward town.

"Cool," said Carlie. "I think Emily wants to come too."

"Do I need to get a permit?"

"No, you can just pay my dad five bucks. He's already gotten several permits."

"I've never gone out and cut down a Christmas tree before," said Morgan. "It sounds like fun."

"We do it every year," said Carlie. "It's kind of a tradition. Hey, have you paid your deposit for the ski trip yet?"

"I have the money now," said Morgan. "But I'll have to wait to do it in the morning when I go to the bazaar."

"Good. It'd be terrible if you didn't go."

Morgan considered this. "Yeah, maybe I should call the church and tell them to save my spot … and that I'll pay tomorrow."

"Yeah," agreed Carlie as they entered their mobile-home park. "You should definitely do that as soon as you get home."

"See ya tomorrow." Morgan waved to Carlie as she turned toward her colorful-looking house. Grandma had already turned on the Christmas lights. Morgan was glad that she'd put them up last night. It made everything look happy and cheerful. Morgan just hoped that Grandma wasn't overdoing it. They had discussed everything at the dinner table last night. And Grandma had promised to take it easy. But when Morgan opened the door, she immediately smelled cookies.

"Grandma?" she called out in a warning tone. "What have you been doing?"

Grandma poked her head out of the kitchen. "What, dear?" she asked innocently.

Morgan looked to see racks of sugar cookies cooling and shook her finger at her grandmother. "You're not supposed to be doing things like this."

Grandma smiled sheepishly. "I just couldn't help myself."

"But Mom said—"

"I know, I know, but I was feeling really spunky. And I had a hankering for some good sugar cookies."

Morgan looked at the messy kitchen and then took Grandma by the arm. "Okay, I promise not to tell Mom if you go and sit down for the rest of the day."

"What about the—"

"I'll clean it up, Grandma. You just go and rest, okay?"

"Well, I guess I can't argue," said Grandma.

"No, you can't."

"I was going to freeze some of those," said Grandma, "to decorate later."

"So how do I do that?" asked Morgan as she helped Grandma to her chair where Grandma gave her step-by-step directions. "That sounds pretty simple," said Morgan. "Anything else?"

"Well, I was hankering after a cup of tea."

"I'll make it," said Morgan firmly. "You just stay here and sit. *Please.*"

Grandma chuckled. "Yes, dear. Whatever you say, dear."

Then Morgan made Grandma some tea and began to clean up the kitchen. By the time everything was cleaned up and put away, it was after four o'clock, and Grandma was happily watching *Oprah*.

"Thank you, honey," she called out as Morgan went to her room.

Morgan looked at the pile of unsewn socks and then at the clock. If she could manage to sew two pairs an hour, she would have them all finished by eleven o'clock. That was if she didn't take any breaks, which wasn't likely. Just the same, it seemed possible, and she set to work. Still, it was slow going. Using the stretchy knit stitch was time consuming. But not using it would ruin the socks. Morgan thought about people in other countries as she sewed. She'd heard stories of children who were forced to work for long hours every day in sweat shops, where they were paid only pennies per hour. At least that wasn't the case with her. Still, the sooner she ended this project the happier she would be. She had always enjoyed sewing and creating, but doing the same thing over and over again was incredibly boring. At least the sock fabric patterns were different.

Morgan sewed until six o'clock, when Mom arrived home with Chinese takeout from Asian Gardens. "Amy said to tell you hi," Mom said as she set the white boxes out on the table. "Boy, were they busy tonight."

"That should make Amy happy," said Morgan. "More tips."

"Are you girls all set for the parade?" asked Grandma. Then Morgan told them about yesterday's fitting and how the elf outfits looked pretty good.

"And how are your socks coming?" asked Mom.

"If I stick with it, I should have them all done in time for the bazaar tomorrow."

"And then you'll bring me what's left?"

"Hopefully there won't be any left," said Morgan with a grin.

After they finished eating, Mom excused Morgan to return to her sewing. "I'll handle cleanup tonight," she told her as she tossed a carton into the trash.

So Morgan returned to sewing. Thanks to things like broken needles, running out of thread, or silly mistakes, it was taking longer than her time estimate. Yet, she was determined not to quit until she was done. It was past midnight when she finally finished the last sock. She turned off the light on the sewing machine and let out a big sigh. Sure, it was hard, but she was done. And hopefully these socks would sell like hotcakes, and she would make enough money in one day to pay for the ski trip and then some.

"Time to get up," called Mom the next morning.

"Huh?" Morgan blinked blurry eyes toward the clock. "Isn't it Saturday?"

"You asked me to wake you up before nine," said Mom.

"Oh, yeah," said Morgan, jumping out of bed. "The bazaar. Can I still get a ride with you?"

"If you can be ready in twenty minutes."

"Yeah, sure." Morgan was already pulling off her pajamas and reaching for her elf costume.

"How is the Queen of Socks?" asked Grandma, poking her head in the doorway.

"All done," said Morgan as she tugged on her tights. "But I haven't had time to make tags or anything."

Grandma came over to look at the pile of socks. "You do nice work, Morgan. Say, maybe I could safety pin the pairs together. Would that help?"

"That'd be awesome," said Morgan as she put on a red turtleneck to wear under the elf costume.

While Morgan dressed and ate a quick breakfast of a banana and milk, Grandma managed to safety pin all the pairs of socks together then put them in a large plastic bag. "Now, maybe you can just make a sign that says eight dollars a pair, and you'll be good to go."

"Great idea." Morgan was stuffing her elf shoes and hat into her backpack. "Thanks, Grandma!"

Grandma frowned. "I just wish I could work at the bazaar today."

"Mother," said Morgan's mom in a stern voice as she pulled on her cape. "We discussed this already. You really must take it easy. There's some leftover Chinese food in the fridge. And I do not want you to do anything except sit in your chair, watch TV, and knit."

"Am I allowed to read?"

"Yes."

Then Morgan and Mom kissed Grandma good-bye and went on their way. Morgan felt sorry for Grandma being stuck at home, but under the circumstances, it seemed the only option.

"I can go home after the Christmas parade," said Morgan. "To be with Grandma, I mean."

"Oh, that would be nice, sweetie. I know she feels bad about missing out on things. Maybe you could tell her how everything went."

"Sure."

Then Mom dropped Morgan at the church. "I'll see you at the Christmas parade," she told her, holding up her camera. "I'm going to close the shop while it's going."

Morgan waved and ran into the church. She headed straight for the office, pulling out her registration form and deposit money. Distracted with cleaning up Grandma's baking mess, she'd forgotten to call yesterday.

"Can I help you?" asked a woman that Morgan didn't recognize.

"Where's Mrs. Albert?" asked Morgan.

"She'll be in later," said the woman.

"Oh." Morgan laid her registration form on the counter and started looking for her money. "I'm registering for the middle-school ski trip."

The woman frowned. "I'm sorry, but that's all full now."

Morgan just stared at her. "Completely full?"

"Yes. And we actually have a waiting list."

"A waiting list?"

The woman nodded. "I don't know if Cory and Janna can take any more kids or not, but I thought it wouldn't hurt to take names." She looked at her paper. "You'll be number three on it."

"Oh…"

"Your name?"

"Uh, Morgan. Morgan Evans."

"Oh, you're Cleo's daughter. Of course." She wrote down the name. "Well, hopefully they'll be able to squeeze a few more in."

Morgan nodded. "Yeah, hopefully." But as she walked through the foyer and on toward the bazaar area, she felt numb. She couldn't believe that she had worked past midnight last night just to sew all these stupid socks, and now she wouldn't even be able to go on the ski trip. What was the point of even selling her socks in here today? All the money made at the bazaar was either to pay their way or to donate to the church's outreach fund. Not that she didn't want to contribute to the outreach fund, but she had twenty pairs of socks in her bag. That was equal to one hundred and sixty dollars. Combined with her fifty dollar deposit, which she had tucked back into her backpack, that would've been more than enough to cover her spot. But now she had no spot.

She blinked back tears as she walked through the sanctuary, which was now serving as the shopping area. Friends from church smiled at her elf costume and said hello to her. She tried to be friendly back, but it was just too hard. Everything felt way too hard. Finally, she got to the youth-group booth, and she knew what she would do. She would donate some of her socks to be used for the outreach fund or whatever. And then she would excuse herself from working there. She would tell them that her grandmother was ill, and that was true — totally true. And then she would walk back home and spend the morning with Grandma.

"Hey, Elf Morgan," called out Emily with a happy smile.

"Hey, Elf Emily," said Morgan, forcing a smile.

"What's the matter?" asked Emily.

"Nothing."

Emily shook her head. "No, I can tell something's wrong, Morgan." She pulled Morgan aside. "What is it?"

"Look, Em," said Morgan quickly. "I can't work here today and — "

"But you have to — "

"No," said Morgan firmly. "My grandma is sick and I need to go — "

"Grandma is sick?" said Emily with concern. "Is it serious?"

"It's her heart."

"Oh no!"

"Anyway, she's going to have surgery next week. And she's not supposed to overdo it or anything ... and I just feel like I should go home and — " Then Morgan began to cry.

"Oh, Morgan," said Emily, wrapping her arms around her and hugging her tightly. "I'm so sorry. Do you want me to come with you?"

"No," said Morgan, wiping her tears with her jacket sleeve. "You stay here and help." She handed Emily the whole bag of socks. Really, what difference did it make if the sock money went completely to the outreach fund? Maybe that was for the best anyway. "They're pinned together. I wanted to sell them for eight dollars a pair."

"Okay." Emily peered at Morgan. "I'll take care of it for you. Tell Grandma hello for me. And let me know if there's anything I can do. I didn't know she was sick, Morgan. I feel so bad."

"It's okay," said Morgan, still sniffing.

"Will you be at the parade?"

"Yeah. I think so. Unless Grandma really needs me."

"Well, don't worry about your socks," said Emily with authority. "I will take care of everything for you."

"Thanks."

Then Emily hugged Morgan again. "I really love you, Morgan. And now I know why you've been acting kind of different. You've been worried about Grandma." She stepped back and shook her head. "And I haven't been a very good friend. I'm sorry."

Now Morgan was starting to cry all over again. "It's okay."

"See you later?"

"Yeah." Before anyone else could ask her what was wrong, Morgan made a quick escape out a side exit. Then she slung her backpack over one shoulder and jogged all the way across town and home.

"What's wrong?" asked Grandma when Morgan came into the house. "I thought you were working at the bazaar."

What Morgan really wanted to do just then was to break into tears and tell Grandma the whole sad story. But she knew that would be wrong. Grandma's heart wasn't strong, and Morgan suspected stress would only make things worse. "There were a lot of people working at the bazaar," she said, which wasn't untrue. "And they didn't really need me. I left my socks with Emily, and she's going to take care of it for me."

"You didn't want to stay and work?" asked Grandma, clearly suspicious.

"I stayed up so late last night," said Morgan as she hung up her jacket. "And there's still the parade ... I was just feeling tired."

Grandma smiled. "Well, I know how that feels."

"And," said Morgan with a smile that she hoped was convincing. "I got to thinking about those sugar cookies, and I only had one yesterday …"

"Hmmm?" Grandma smiled. "That would be nice with a cup of tea now, wouldn't it?"

"It sure would. You sit down and I'll get it ready."

And so Grandma and Morgan enjoyed a nice little tea party, just the two of them. And then they both took a morning nap. Morgan felt surprisingly better when she woke up a little before noon. Oh, sure, she was still bummed about not getting to go on the ski trip, but she wasn't going to let that ruin her life. Besides, she told herself, maybe it was better this way. Maybe Grandma was going to need Morgan at home, after her surgery and everything.

"Are you going to the parade?" asked Grandma as she looked at the clock.

"Will you promise to be good while I'm gone?" said Morgan.

"I promise," said Grandma. "Your mother said she'd take pictures on her new digital camera and show them to me tonight. I want to see my granddaughter elf with her friends."

"Okay, then," said Morgan. "Just make sure you keep your promise."

"And you promise to have fun," said Grandma. "You've been working too hard lately."

"Okay," said Morgan. "I will have fun."

"I wish I could offer you a ride to — "

"Grandma," said Morgan in a warning tone.

"I know ..."

Morgan didn't even mind walking back to town. There seemed to be no sign of rain, and the cool breeze was kind of invigorating. But the best part was that, as she walked, she prayed. She told God that she was okay about not going on the ski trip and that her faith was big enough to trust him despite feeling disappointed. But mostly she prayed about Grandma. She begged God to make the surgery go well, and for Grandma to be her happy and energetic old self again. That meant more to Morgan than anything.

chapter ten

"You're here!" Emily cried, hugging Morgan as she joined the others in the staging area. "I told them about your grandma and everything."

The other girls all expressed their concern, and Morgan was afraid she was going to start crying all over again. She wondered why sympathy did that to a person. But before long she was distracted with getting her elf shoes and elf hat on properly, and then they were all taking their places on the float and listening to Mrs. Landers' instructions.

"Just dance or sing or whatever you feel like doing," she told them. "The music should be fun, and mostly we just want you to look like happy elves." She gave them bags of candy to toss to the kids. "Just don't throw it too hard," she warned them. "We don't want Santa's elves putting any eyes out."

Soon they were taking off, and Morgan found that she was actually keeping her promise to Grandma. She was having fun. It was fun being on the float with her best friends, and she felt thankful to have them. She even spotted Mom standing in front of Cleopatra's with Maureen.

She waved and smiled and tossed them candy as Mom took photos. And before long, it was all over — and a good thing since it was just starting to rain.

"As a thank you to the elves, who were brilliant," said Mrs. Landers as they climbed off the float, "I am taking you all out for lunch."

Morgan considered joining them, but she still felt concerned for Grandma. "I think I should go home," she told them as she removed the elf shoes and put her boots back on. "Mom has to work all day, and Grandma is alone." Fortunately, they understood and didn't pressure her to come. And when no one was looking, she grabbed her backpack and headed home.

Grandma was napping, and Morgan went to her room to remove the now soggy elf costume. She hung it up, put on some cozy sweats, and then flopped down on her bed and started to read a book. But just as she turned a page, she heard a crashing sound in the living room. She jumped up and went out in time to see Grandma's TV tray splattered across the living room floor and Grandma standing in front of her recliner and clutching her chest.

"Grandma," said Morgan in a surprisingly calm voice. "Let me help you." She quickly eased Grandma back in her chair and fully reclined it, putting Grandma's feet up. "Are those your pills?" asked Morgan as she grabbed up a prescription bottle.

"Yes," gasped Grandma.

Morgan opened the bottle and gave Grandma a pill, running to the kitchen for water and the cordless phone. Then as she handed Grandma the water, she dialed 911 and waited.

"It's my grandmother," Morgan said, "I think she's having a heart attack." Then Morgan told the man on the phone their address.

"Keep her lying down," said the man. "Does she have any heart medicine or aspirin handy?"

"She is lying down," said Morgan. "And she just took a pill. Should I get aspirin too?"

"Now don't hang up, but can you tell me what kind of pill?"

So Morgan read the name from the bottle, and the man said, "You don't need to give her aspirin; that pill should help. Paramedics are on the way. Is your grandmother conscious?"

Morgan looked down at Grandma. She was lying so still, with her eyes closed. "I don't know." She put her hand on Grandma's cheek, and her eyelashes fluttered. "Hurry," said Morgan into the phone. "Please, hurry!"

"The ambulance is on its way. Just stay on the phone."

Morgan kneeled next to Grandma with the phone still in her hand. "Dear God," she prayed. "I need you to help Grandma right now. Please, please, God, help her to be okay. Help her heart to be okay. Help the ambulance to get here soon. Take care of her for me, God. I love my grandma so much. Please, don't take her away. We need her." Just then Morgan heard the sound of a siren, and soon the paramedics were in the house, tending to Grandma. Morgan just stood in the background, still praying.

"She's stabilized and ready for transport," said a woman paramedic to Morgan. "Are you the only one at home?"

Morgan just nodded.

"Want to ride in the ambulance?"

With tears in her eyes, Morgan nodded again and followed them as they rolled the gurney with Grandma on it out the door. She sat up in front with the driver. He told her not to worry, that these paramedics were the best, and that it looked like her grandmother would be fine. Morgan told him that Grandma was supposed to have heart surgery next week.

"Well, I'll bet that surgery date just got moved up," he said.

At the hospital, Grandma was taken to the emergency room, and Morgan called her mother from the waiting room.

"Oh, my goodness," said Mom. "I'm so glad you were home, honey. I'll be right there."

It seemed to take forever for Mom to get there, but Morgan tried to make good use of the time by praying. Then she remembered the church's prayer chain and called the office and quickly relayed the emergency. "We'll be right on it," said a voice that sounded like the same woman who had put Morgan's name on the waiting list that morning. "We'll be praying hard."

"Morgan," said Mom as she burst into the waiting room. "How is she?"

"I don't know," said Morgan. "They told me to stay here. They said they'd let me know. It's been almost an hour."

"I'll go ask."

Morgan followed Mom to the desk where the receptionist seemed to know little. But Mom wouldn't give up without an answer, and they waited until an ER doctor finally came out to speak to them. "They're prepping her for surgery right now," he said. "Lucky for her, one of our best heart surgeons, Dr. Cowden, just happened to be on hand this afternoon. And fortunately we have all her test results from last week, and we've spoken to her GP. They should be taking her into surgery within the hour."

"Oh, my," said Mom. "Do you know how long the surgery will last?"

"Hard to say. They won't know until they go in whether she needs a valve replacement or a valve repair."

"Which is better?"

"If the valve isn't too severely damaged, it's usually preferable to repair it. The human body has amazing abilities to heal. A valve replacement can involve some other challenges like anti-coagulation therapy."

Most of this was going straight over Morgan's head. All she knew was that she had better keep praying. And the more people praying, the better.

"I already called the church prayer chain," Morgan told Mom as they returned to the waiting area. "But I'm going to call my friends too."

She called Emily's number, quickly relaying the events of the afternoon. "I just thought maybe you guys could be praying for her," Morgan said finally.

"Of course," said Emily. "I'm going babysitting again in a little bit, but I'll try to pray as much as I can. And I'll call Amy and Carlie and Chelsea and ask them to pray too."

"Thanks."

"It's a good thing you went home when you did, wasn't it?"

"More like a God thing."

"Definitely. Oh, by the way, I went back to the bazaar this afternoon and all of your socks had sold."

"Good."

"Yeah, I'm sure that seems unimportant in light of this."

"Sort of ..."

"Well, I'll call the others. We'll all be praying."

"Thanks."

"I love you, Morgan. And I'm going to be a better friend."

"Thanks, Em. I love you too."

The next few hours were the longest ones in Morgan's life. Several church members joined them, and eventually they all went to the hospital chapel where they bowed their heads and prayed. Then, finally, just before nine o'clock, Dr. Cowden came to speak to them.

"It went as well as it could possibly go," he told them. "We were able to repair the mitral valve, rather than replacing it. The rest of her heart appeared to be in good shape."

"That's good to hear," said Mom.

"She's in recovery for the next hour and will be moved to ICU after that."

"Can we see her?" asked Mom.

"Not until she's in ICU," he said. "And then only immediate family, one at a time, and not for more than five minutes."

Mom tried to get Morgan to go home with one of their church friends, but Morgan refused. "I'm staying as long as you're staying," she informed her mother.

It was past ten o'clock before Mom got to go in and see Grandma. Morgan waited nervously in the hallway, hoping she too would get a turn.

"Grandma wants to see you," Mom said as she came out. "But keep it short, she needs to rest."

Morgan nodded and quietly tiptoed into Grandma's room, going over to stand by her bed. There were tubes and wires everywhere, but Morgan focused her eyes on her grandmother's face. "I love you, Grandma," she whispered.

Grandma's eyes opened. "I love you too, darling," she said in a husky voice.

"Don't talk," said Morgan. "I don't want to wear you out. I just want to say that I know you're going to be okay, Grandma. Everyone is praying for you, and your surgery went really well, and I just know you're going to be okay."

Grandma smiled, and Morgan knew that it was true. She was going to be okay.

"I'm not supposed to stay too long." Morgan reached over and put her hand on Grandma's. "But I'll see you tomorrow. Rest well, okay."

"You too," whispered Grandma.

Grandma was better the next day. She wasn't getting out of bed just yet, but she could talk a bit and listen a while. Morgan and Mom went to see her first thing in the morning and then again later in the afternoon.

"I went with Carlie to get a tree today," Morgan told her. "It was so fun. We went out in the woods, and I cut it down all by myself. Mr. Garcia let me use his saw. Then I dragged it all the way back to the truck by myself. It's not a real big tree, but it looks good in our house. I put it where you always do, but I didn't have time to put decorations on it yet. It smells so good, Grandma." Then Morgan put her hands close to Grandma's face. "Maybe you can smell it too. I think I still have pine pitch on my hands."

Grandma sniffed and then smiled. "Mmm … it smells just like Christmas."

"It does, doesn't it?"

By Monday, Grandma was moved from ICU to a regular room, and the plan was to release her by Saturday. "She's doing really well," Mom told Morgan as they drove to the hospital that evening. "The doctor told me that she'll need to take it nice and easy when she comes home, but that it won't be long, probably sometime after the New Year, and she can start resuming her old routines."

"Maybe it's a good thing I'm not going on the ski trip."

"You're not going?"

Morgan realized that she'd never told Mom about her disappointment. It seemed so small now compared to everything else. "I tried to sign up too late," she told her. "But it's okay."

"Oh, I'm sorry, sweetie. But I thought all your socks got sold at the bazaar. Wasn't that supposed to be your ski trip money?"

"I think it'll go to the outreach fund."

Mom stopped at the stoplight and turned to look at Morgan. "And you're okay with that?"

"Sure. That fund is to help people who really need it."

The light turned green, and Mom continued to drive through town. "Oh, I almost forgot, I sold all of your socks at the store too. You'll never guess who came and bought the last two pairs."

"Who?"

"Old Miss McPhearson." Mom chuckled.

"And you still had the right sizes left for her?"

"I don't know. I explained that one pair was a large and one was a small, but she didn't seem to care. She bought them both."

Morgan laughed. "Well, I guess she can always give them away."

"So, do you think you'll make any more socks, Morgan? I know I could probably sell lots of them."

"I don't know." Morgan just shook her head. "I think I got kinda burned out on it."

"Maybe Grandma will feel like taking it over for you. I mean, when she's back to normal again."

"Yeah," said Morgan as they pulled into the hospital. "She's welcome to it."

The next few days passed like a flash. With the Christmas concert and Christmas parties and the last days of school before winter break, combined with visiting Grandma in the hospital every afternoon, and taking care of things at home, Morgan could hardly believe it when it was Friday and Grandma was actually coming home the next day. Morgan had put off decorating the Christmas tree until Grandma was home. Her plan was to set Grandma up in her recliner so she could watch as Morgan decorated.

"I'd be lost without you," Mom told Morgan on Saturday night after they'd put Grandma to bed. They were in the kitchen, cleaning up the dinner things.

"Ditto," said Morgan.

"No, I mean it. And it's such a blessing that you're on winter break now — you know this is my busiest time of year in the shop. I'd be in trouble if you couldn't help out. Although I feel bad to have you stuck at home during your vacation time."

"I already told you, Mom, I'm fine with this. I'll do some beading and make some Christmas presents, and maybe Emily will want to come over some of the time. Really, I'm just glad that Grandma is okay … that she's home."

"You know I was thinking about everything," Mom said as she dried a platter. "God's hand was really on us through all of this."

"I know." Morgan thought about the day when she came home early from the parade, trying to remember what made her decline the invitation to hang with her friends and go to lunch. "You know what?" she said suddenly.

"What?"

"Well, it was last Saturday when I found out that I was too late for the ski trip registration. I was so bummed — that's why I came home early, and that's why I was here when Grandma had her heart attack."

"God does work in mysterious ways, doesn't he?" said Mom.

"Yeah, he really does bring good out of bad."

"And you're really okay with not going?"

"I am, Mom. I mean, sure, it was a disappointment. But I'm okay."

chapter eleven

Grandma steadily grew stronger, and by the middle of the following week, she was able to sit out in her recliner for several hours at a time. After lunch, she asked Morgan about the tree. "It's pretty like it is," she said, "But don't you want to decorate it?"

"Yeah," said Morgan. "I thought you might enjoy supervising while I decorate it."

"Why don't you invite Emily over to help you?" suggested Grandma.

"That would be okay? It wouldn't wear you out or anything?"

"As long as you don't make me get up and dance a Christmas jig, I think I should be fine."

So Morgan called Emily and asked her to come over.

"I'd love to come over," Emily said. "I've been wanting to call you, but I was worried I might disturb your grandma."

"Grandma asked for you to come over."

"She did?"

"She wants us to decorate the tree."

"Cool. I'm on my way."

"Do we have any more of those sugar cookies?" asked Grandma.

"Of course," said Morgan, "You made dozens of them, and I put them in the freezer just like you said."

"Maybe you and Emily could decorate some of them … after the tree."

"Maybe we could put on our elf outfits," said Morgan.

Grandma chuckled. "Now, wouldn't that be cute."

Under Grandma's supervision, Emily and Morgan decorated the tree. Then they decorated the cookies and took a plate out to show Grandma.

"Those are beautiful," said Grandma. "Too pretty to eat."

"No, they're not," said Morgan. "Take one and try it."

So Grandma took a Santa and bit off his head. "This would be good with a cup of tea," she said as she munched. After tea and cookies, Grandma turned on *Oprah*, and Emily and Morgan went to Morgan's room to work on beads.

"Did I tell you how much money I made babysitting?" asked Emily as she threaded her needle.

"No." Morgan strung a bright red glass bead next to a silver one and studied it for a moment to see if she liked how it looked. This necklace was going to be for Mom, and she wanted it to be perfect.

"In just two nights I made two hundred and twenty dollars."

"No way."

"I know, it was amazing. But it's just because of these Christmas parties that last really late, and I watched kids for two couples each night. It was a little hairy at first because there were like six kids one night. But after they all went to sleep, all I had to do was sit and watch TV. The parents didn't get home until like two in the morning. And then they both paid ten bucks an hour, plus a tip."

"Too bad they don't have Christmas parties all the time."

"Well, they already asked me about New Year's Eve."

"Did you say yes?"

"I said, maybe, if I had help. I thought you might want to try it with me."

"What about Chelsea?"

"She doesn't like little kids."

"Oh ..."

"Chelsea's a lot nicer than I used to think," said Emily.

"Yeah, it seems like she's changing."

"But she's not the same as you, Morgan."

"Well, everyone is different."

"You know what I mean."

Morgan turned to look at Emily. "What do you mean?"

"I mean you're my best friend, Morgan. I hope I'm still your best friend."

"Yeah, of course."

"And we're going to have such a cool time on the ski trip."

"Well, I ..."

"Oh, yeah!" Emily sat up straight. "I almost forgot. I was going to teach you to skateboard. Well, we still have more than a week. That's plenty of time."

"You don't need to—"

"No, I want to teach you, Morgan. It'll be fun, and I know you'll be good at it. You just need to practice a little before the ski trip."

"That's the deal, Em." Morgan sighed. "I'm not going on the ski trip."

"Not going?" Emily just stared at her.

"Yeah. I'm not going."

Emily frowned now. "Oh, is it because of your grandma? Because my mom already offered to come over here while we're gone. She isn't working that week anyway, and she really likes your grandma. She was going to call your mom and offer and—"

"No," said Morgan. "It's not because of Grandma. It's because I didn't get signed up in time."

Now Emily looked confused. "Yeah, you did."

"No, I didn't. The trip was full when I went in to the church office."

"Did you talk to Mrs. Albert?"

"No, she wasn't there."

"So how do you know you're not signed up?"

"Because I got put on the waiting list."

"That's impossible."

"It's the truth, Emily."

"Can I use your phone?" asked Emily.

"Why?"

"To check something."

"Yeah, whatever." Now Morgan was starting to feel bummed again. She had already accepted the fact that she was going to miss out, but having Emily acting like this wasn't helping much. Morgan stayed in her room while Emily made her phone call.

"Okay," said Emily as she came back and flopped down on Morgan's bean bag chair. "It's settled."

"What's settled?"

"You are going."

"Where?"

"On the ski trip, Morgan. You *are* going."

"How is that even possible?"

"Well, I wasn't supposed to say anything ... but under the circumstances, I think it's okay to tell you."

"To tell me what?" Morgan felt impatient now. What was going on?

"You were already signed up for the trip, Morgan. Your deposit was all paid, and they were just waiting for you to turn in your registration form, which you apparently did on Saturday, when you thought you were put on the waiting list."

"Huh?" Morgan shook her head, still trying to make sense of this.

"And you made enough money selling socks at the bazaar to cover the rest with some leftover to go to the outreach fund."

"I don't get it. *Who* paid my deposit?" asked Morgan.

"I wasn't supposed to say, but I think it's okay. Chelsea and I were worried that you weren't going to make it on time. And Chelsea's mom heard us talking, and she was so pleased with what you'd done with the elf skirts that she wanted to pay your deposit as a thank you."

"Really?" Morgan hadn't expected this.

"Yeah. Don't tell her I told you, okay?"

"So, I really am going on the ski trip?" Morgan stood now with her arms outstretched, she felt like she was about to jump up and down with joy.

"Yes!" Emily hugged her. "You really are going!"

Now Morgan was jumping. And Emily was jumping too. Morgan hugged her best friend. "Thank you!" she cried as she continued to jump and dance around the room. "Thank you, thank you, thank you!"

"Don't thank me," said Emily.

Morgan paused. "And I can't thank Chelsea's mom—"

"Maybe you should just thank God," suggested Emily.

Morgan closed her eyes and tilted her head up.

"Thank you, God!" she said joyfully. But even as she said it, she knew that she wasn't just thanking him for the ski trip — she was thanking him for *everything*!

Run Away

chapter one

"What do you mean I can't go on the ski trip?" Emily asked her mom for the third time. "I earned all my money and I'm all registered and I—"

"It doesn't have to do with any of that," said Mom as she jerked a suitcase from the shelf in her closet, dusted it off, and then tossed it onto her bed.

"And why are you getting that out?" demanded Emily. "Are you going somewhere?"

"We're *all* going somewhere," said Mom. "I want you to go to your room and pack."

"Are we going somewhere for Christmas?" asked Emily, still confused. It was less than a week before Christmas, and this was the first she'd heard of a trip.

"Something like that," said Mom quickly. "Just do as I say and I'll explain later."

"But what about Kyle?" asked Emily. "Isn't he going too?"

"Yes. I'll have to pack for him. He's still at work. We'll pick him up on our way out."

"What am I supposed to pack?" asked Emily, hoping that they might be going somewhere fun.

"Everything," said Mom as she pulled open a drawer.

"What do you mean *everything*?"

"I mean everything that you brought when we moved here last spring. And anything you bought since then. Don't pack any of the things that Morgan's family loaned us. Those will have to be returned … later."

"Returned?"

"Oh, Emily," said Mom in her exasperated voice as she tossed a handful of socks and underclothes into her bag. "I don't have time for questions right now. We need to get moving — and out of here — fast!"

Emily stared at her mom in horror. "Are we leaving — I mean moving — for good?"

"I'm sorry, Emily. I wish it wasn't true."

"But … but … why?" Emily felt a lump like a hard rock growing in her throat.

"It's your father …"

"Dad?"

"Yes …" Mom stood up straight and, pushing a strand of blonde hair from her eyes, she looked at Emily with an expression that Emily remembered from back in the old days, back before they moved to Boscoe Bay. "I just found out that he knows where we are."

"How would he know? How did you find that out?"

"I just happened to call your Aunt Becky this morning. I used a friend's cell phone at work, so it couldn't be traced back … I just wanted to wish her a Merry Christmas." Mom carried a bunch of clothes from her closet and tossed them onto the already crowded bed. "Becky told me that your dad hired a private investigator who somehow tracked us down. She said that he is on his way here right now. So, don't you see, Emily? We have to get out of here — immediately!"

"But why do *we* have to be the ones to run away?" pleaded Emily. "We haven't done anything wrong!"

"I know." Mom sighed loudly.

"He's the one who should be running, Mom. He's the one who's done all the bad stuff."

"I know … I know …" Mom sighed loudly. "There's no time to talk about this now. Just go pack, Emily. Hurry."

"But, Mom!" Emily pleaded with her. "I have friends here. I have a life and I don't want to — "

"Neither do I, Emily. But it's what we *have* to do. I told you and Kyle, right from the start, that our stay in Boscoe Bay might be brief."

"But what does that mean, Mom?" asked Emily in desperation. "That we'll have to keep running and running forever?"

"I don't know …" Mom closed her eyes and shook her head. "All I know is that we need to get out of here right *now.*" She narrowed her eyes and gave Emily a look that said "I am dead serious, and I want no argument."

"Okay," said Emily as she went to her room. Tears were filling her eyes as she began to gather her things and pile them on the futon bed that Morgan had loaned to her when they first came here. It was funny … she'd come to think of that bed, as well as so many other things, as her own. Suddenly it seemed as if nothing was really hers. Not her home or her school … and worst of all, not her friends.

"Here," said Mom after a few minutes. "Just stuff your things into these." She tossed several large black trash bags into Emily's bedroom. "I'm going to pack for Kyle now."

Before long, Emily was done, but Mom was still gathering things up. "Can I go tell Morgan that I'm leaving?" Emily asked sadly.

Mom frowned. "I don't know …"

"But they're going to wonder what happened to us," Emily persisted. "We were supposed to go to their house for Christmas. And I was supposed to meet the girls at the clubhouse this afternoon. They might think we've been abducted or something. And, knowing Morgan, she might even call the police."

Mom nodded. "Yes. You're right. They've been good friends to us. And we can trust them. Go ahead and tell them that we're leaving this afternoon. I've already explained things to Mr. Greeley. Tell Mrs. Evans that Mr. Greeley can give her the house key so that they can come collect their — their things." Mom's voice broke and tears came streaming down her cheeks now.

"Oh, Mom," said Emily, running over to hug her. "This is so horrible."

"I know," said Mom as she ran her hand over Emily's hair. "I wish there was another way."

"Why isn't there?" asked Emily.

Mom just shook her head. "I don't know …" Then Mom turned back to packing Kyle's things.

"I'm going to Morgan's," said Emily as she grabbed her jacket.

"Don't stay long," warned Mom. "I'm almost ready to go right now, and if you don't get back here in time, I'll just drive over there and honk — and you better come a-running."

"Okay."

Emily picked up Morgan's Christmas present. It wasn't much, just a leopard-print picture frame with a photo of her and Morgan in it. The gift wasn't even wrapped, but Emily didn't want to miss the chance to give it to her. Also, she'd have to ask Morgan to give the gifts (the things she and Morgan had been working on the past few days) to their other friends for her.

"Hey, Em," said Morgan happily as she opened the door. "I'm so glad you're here. I've got something I want to show you."

Emily stepped into Morgan's living room as Morgan dashed off toward her bedroom. Emily looked around the cozy house, trying to memorize every single thing about this place in one quick glance. The happy clutter of Grandma's homemade afghans and worn furniture mixed with the more eclectic style of Morgan's mom's art and nicer things. From the first time Emily had stepped through their front door, she had always felt welcome here.

"Hello, Emily," called Grandma from her recliner.

"How are you feeling today?" asked Emily as she approached her. Morgan's grandma had recently undergone some very serious heart surgery and had only been sitting up for a few days now.

"I'm feeling right as rain," said Grandma.

"I'm glad." Emily forced a smile as she looked down at her.

Grandma frowned. "But what about you, honey? You don't look too well to me."

"Oh, I'm a little sad," said Emily. *What an understatement.*

"*Sad?*" Grandma peered curiously at her. "Whatever for?"

"Yeah?" said Morgan as she reappeared wearing an interesting hat that appeared to have been patchworked together from scraps of polar fleece — probably the leftovers from her recent sock-sewing project. "What's up, Em?"

Emily tried to blink back the tears, but it was impossible. "We have to … have to leave."

Morgan frowned. "You mean you guys are going somewhere for Christmas? I thought you were going to come to
our house for —"

"No, I mean, I mean we have to leave … for … for
good!" Now Emily was crying full force.

"*Why?*" cried Morgan, running over and putting her
arms around Emily.

"Yes, why?" said Grandma more calmly.

Emily worked hard to recover from her outburst,
finally taking a tissue from Grandma's hand. "Thanks."

"Now, sit down on the sofa there and tell us exactly
what's going on," Grandma commanded her.

"Well …" Emily took in a slow breath. "You know a
little bit about why we came here. You guys and Mr. Greeley are the only ones who know about …"

"You mean about your father?" supplied Grandma.

"Yes." Emily nodded. "I guess he's found out where we
are."

"*So?*" said Morgan in a defiant tone. It was actually
sort of how Emily felt herself when Mom first told her the
news.

"So … my mom says that means we have to go."

"But why?" demanded Morgan. Her dark eyes were
filling with tears too.

"I don't really know …" Emily looked down at her
hands in her lap. "I guess it's because Mom thinks he

might hurt us again."

"But how can he hurt you?" asked Morgan. "I mean what about police protection and things like that?"

"I don't know …" Emily just shook her head.

"Morgan does have a point," said Grandma. "Running away might not solve your problem, Emily. Sometimes it's better to stay and fight for your rights. You and your family have good friends here in the mobile-home park, as well as at church. You have a community that could stand behind you and protect you. If you're out someplace new, where people don't know you … well, that might be less safe."

Emily looked up at Grandma's kind brown face and nodded. "Yes, yes … that makes sense."

"It does," said Morgan. "I mean, what if you guys were out on the road, staying at a hotel or something, and your dad found you there? Which would be worse?"

Emily considered this. "I know what you mean." Then she thought of her mother. "But for some reason Mom doesn't see it that way."

"But *why?*" cried Morgan. "It just seems so wrong that your family should have to be on the run from your dad. *Why? Why? Why?*"

Just then, Emily heard Mom's car horn honking out front. "I've got to go," she said quickly. "Mom said to tell you that Mr. Greeley has the key to our house and you guys can go over there whenever you want to get your things." She held out her gift for Morgan. "This was going to be your Christmas present." Again came the honking sound. "I didn't have time to wrap it."

"But, Emily—"

"I've got to go," said Emily.

"I'm not even done with your present yet," said Morgan. Then she pulled the brightly colored hat from her head and shoved it onto Emily's head. "Here, take this for now." Then she hugged her again. "I don't want you to leave."

"I don't want to leave."

"You're my best friend ever," cried Morgan.

"You're mine too!" sobbed Emily.

This time Mom's horn honked loud and long.

"You better go, honey," said Grandma. "But please tell your mom what we said. And if there is anything we can do—I mean anything at all—please, call us. Remember you have your friends, the church, the community here … there's a lot of power in those kinds of numbers."

"I'll tell Mom." Emily ran over and quickly hugged Grandma. "Thanks … for everything."

"You be sure and call us, Emily," said Grandma. "And you can call collect if you need to. And don't forget that wherever you go God is with you. And we are praying for you."

"Yes," said Morgan. "And this isn't over yet. I'm going to pray for God to bring you back here to us, Emily."

"We'll all be praying for that," called Grandma.

Emily thanked them again, then went out the door just as Mom began to honk the horn one more time. It was starting to rain as Emily ran out to the car. She wished that what Morgan and Grandma were saying could really be true — she wished it was possible for them to pray her and her family back here to Harbor View. But as she got into the car, she couldn't forget the last time their family had to run, leaving their home and everything behind. They never did go back then. Why would this time be any different?

chapter two

"We have an emergency," said Morgan when all the girls were finally seated in the clubhouse.

"Where's Emily?" asked Chelsea.

"Exactly," said Morgan. "That's the emergency."

"Did she get hurt?" asked Amy.

"No." Then, since there seemed to be no reason to keep this thing secret any longer, Morgan explained why Emily's family had to flee so suddenly this afternoon.

"Wow," said Chelsea. "I had no idea."

"Poor Emily," said Carlie.

"That's crazy," said Amy. "Why should Emily's family have to run away from a dad who treated them like that?"

"That's what I think too," said Morgan.

"They need a lawyer," said Chelsea.

"I'm sure they can't afford one," said Morgan.

"My dad has a friend who's a lawyer," said Chelsea. "In fact, Emily babysat for them to earn money for the ski trip."

"This means Emily is going to miss the ski trip," said Amy sadly.

"Not if we can help them," said Morgan.

"How can we help them?" asked Carlie.

"Do we even know how to reach them?" asked Chelsea.

Morgan considered this. "Not really."

"Then how can we help them?" asked Amy.

"By praying," said Morgan. "We'll start by praying."

So, right then and there, all four girls bowed their heads and prayed for Emily and her family. They prayed for God to protect them and to get them safely back to Boscoe Bay and Harbor View.

"Amen," said Morgan when they'd finished.

The girls sat quietly in the bus for about a minute. All they could hear was the sound of the Oregon rain beating down on the roof of the bus.

"So, I guess this means our Christmas party is off," said Amy sadly.

"I know I don't feel much like a party," said Morgan.

"Me neither," added Carlie.

"I'm calling my dad," said Chelsea as she opened up her cell phone.

"Why?" asked Morgan.

"I'm going to ask him to talk to Mr. Lawrence. He's a lawyer, and Dad can ask him if he can figure out a way to help Emily's family."

"Great," said Morgan.

"But even if Mr. Lawrence is willing to help them . . . how do we let Emily's mom know about it?" asked Amy.

"Yeah," said Carlie, "it seems pretty impossible."

"I guess we'll just have to keep praying," said Morgan. "Because God is the only one I know who can do what's impossible."

"And we'll do whatever we can to help," said Carlie.

Morgan held up her arm with the rainbows rule bracelet. "All for one, and one for all?"

The other girls, including Chelsea — who was talking to her dad now — held up their arms in unison.

"I know, Daddy," said Chelsea. "But this *is* an emergency." Then she told him about Emily's situation, painting a dramatic account of how Emily's family was, right this minute, fleeing in fear for their own safety. Chelsea listened for a minute or two. "Yes," she said with excitement. "That's exactly what I thought too. They need a lawyer. What about Mr. Lawrence?" She waited again. "You will, Daddy?" She smiled happily at her friends now. "Thanks so much! Yes, I'll leave my phone on. Thank you, Daddy!" Then she closed her phone.

"Is he going to talk to the lawyer?"

"Yep."

"But, even if he talks to the lawyer," Amy reminded them, "we don't know how to reach Emily right now."

"That's why we have to keep praying," said Morgan.

They called their meeting to a close earlier than usual, and all of them promised to keep praying for Emily.

"Can I stay at your house until my mom gets here?" Chelsea asked Morgan as they started trudging down the wet sandy trail back to the mobile-home park.

"Sure," said Morgan.

Although it was still raining, all four girls paused briefly in front of Emily's now abandoned house. They just stood there looking sadly at it.

"This isn't over yet," proclaimed Morgan.

Now Chelsea stuck her hand with the bracelet on it in the air. "Here's to rescuing Emily," she said.

"To rescuing Emily," echoed Morgan, and the others joined in. Then they ran off to their houses.

Once Morgan and Chelsea were inside the house, and before they even removed their wet jackets, Chelsea was calling her mom to ask her to pick her up. "We quit early," she told her, explaining about Emily's family's unexpected departure. "Daddy is calling Mr. Lawrence right now," she said. "We're all going to do whatever we can to get Emily back here."

"Excuse me for eavesdropping," said Grandma as the girls came into the living room. "But who is Mr. Lawrence?"

Morgan told Grandma about Chelsea's idea, and Grandma smiled. "Yes," she said. "That's exactly how a community should work. People helping one another."

"Do you want a Christmas cookie?" asked Morgan. "Emily and I decorated them just the other day."

"Sure," said Chelsea, following Morgan into the kitchen.

"Want some too?" Morgan called out to Grandma. "And some tea?"

Soon the three of them were back in the living room having cookies and tea and discussing ways they might be able to find out where Emily's family was.

"You have to give your license plate numbers when you stay at a hotel," Chelsea said between bites. "I know, because my mom never can remember hers, and I usually have to run out and check."

"But we don't know Emily's mom's license number," said Morgan. "At least I don't."

"Me neither," said Chelsea. "Do you have any idea which way they were going? North, south, east, or west?"

"Not west," said Morgan. "That would be straight into the Pacific Ocean."

"And I doubt they're going east," said Chelsea, "if they originally ran away from Idaho like you said."

"My guess is south," said Grandma as she set her teacup down.

"Why?" asked Morgan.

"A couple of reasons … one, it's warmer down there in the winter time, and two, there are more people down in California, it's probably easier to disappear."

"That's true," said Chelsea. "It's a lot more crowded down there than up here."

"We need a map," said Morgan suddenly. "A road map."

"There's one in my car," said Grandma. "In the glove compartment."

So Morgan dashed out to the carport and returned with a map, which she soon had spread across the coffee table. "So," she began, "if they're going south, they might be on this highway right here." She looked at the clock. "They left almost two hours ago." She glanced at Grandma. "How fast do you think they're driving on this highway?"

"Not more than sixty miles an hour," said Grandma. "That's a curvy road, and the weather isn't very good for driving."

Morgan checked the key on the map and did some quick figuring. "Well, Emily's mom still had to pick up Kyle, so that used up some time. So if they've been on the road for, say, an hour and a half, maybe that means they're about here by now."

"Hey, that's pretty good," said Chelsea. "Do you really think so?"

Morgan shrugged. "If Grandma is right and they're really going south."

Just then, they heard a horn honking. Morgan jumped to her feet, dashing to the window, thinking that it was Emily's mom again. But it was just Mrs. Landers in her

Mercedes. "Your mom is here," Morgan called back to Chelsea.

Chelsea tugged on her still-wet parka.

"Well, let's keep in touch," said Chelsea. "We need to do everything we can to get Emily back here."

"And let's keep praying," Morgan reminded her.

"Absolutely," said Chelsea. Then Chelsea did something that Morgan couldn't ever remember her doing before. She reached out and hugged Morgan. "I'm glad we're friends, Morgan."

Morgan nodded. "Me too."

"And somehow we're going to get Emily back here."

"See ya," called Morgan as Chelsea dashed out into the rain.

Morgan closed the door and went back to where Grandma was just finishing up her tea. "Chelsea seems like a nice girl," said Grandma.

"Yeah," agreed Morgan. "I've had my doubts sometimes, but I think you're right. She really is a nice girl."

Grandma chuckled. "I suppose that some people can be just as prejudiced against rich people as others are prejudiced against black people."

Morgan sighed. "Yeah, I suppose so."

"Aren't you glad that God sees past all that?"

"That's for sure," said Morgan as she cleaned up the tea things.

"Well, I suppose I should go have a little rest," said Grandma.

"Need any help?" offered Morgan.

"No, honey, I'm fine. I feel stronger every day."

Morgan thought about Emily as she rinsed off the plates and cups in the kitchen sink. She wondered if her calculations about their road trip were even close. Was Emily's car really about a hundred miles south of Boscoe Bay right now? Were they still driving along the Oregon coast highway, wipers slapping against the windshield so that they could see their way through this rain? She wondered how Emily and her brother were feeling just now. Were they all talking? Or was the car silent and somber? She imagined the three of them packed in there between all their personal belongings. Was it cramped? Surely Emily must feel as if her whole life had just been jerked out from under her — all over again. Her family would have to relocate, get started in new schools, get new jobs. It was overwhelming for Morgan to even try to wrap her head around it. And what about Christmas, which was less than a week away? Where would they be by then? In some shabby motel room? Morgan couldn't imagine how she would feel if she were in Emily's shoes. Poor Emily!

Out of habit, Morgan reached up to finger one of her beaded braids. It was something she did when she was feeling anxious about something. And then she would pray about whatever was bothering her. But, as she touched a soft curl, she remembered that the beaded braids were gone, and she instantly wished that she'd never gotten her hair changed. What had she been thinking? Of course, she knew exactly what she'd been thinking. She'd been jealous of the developing friendship between Emily and Chelsea. She had wanted to look less her African-American self and more like them. How totally stupid! And now Emily was gone and Morgan actually was starting to like Chelsea much better. Grandma was right. Morgan had been wrong about Chelsea. Funny how life could change like that — so quickly.

As Morgan stood there, she was looking directly across the road at Mr. Greeley's house. Suddenly she remembered something that Emily had said about Mr. Greeley, about him knowing that Emily's family was leaving and having a key to their house so they could pick up their things. Well, some of the things at Emily's belonged to Morgan — although, in her heart, she had given them to Emily. Still, it provided a good excuse to go snoop around. And maybe she could uncover something that would help them locate Emily. Something that could help bring Emily and her family back here — back where they belonged!

chapter three

No one spoke in the car for quite awhile. Emily knew that
they were all feeling very sad about leaving Boscoe Bay.
Kyle had put up a lot of protest when Mom picked him
up at the gas station where he'd been working these past
few months. Kyle even suggested that he might stay behind
and live with a friend, but Mom wouldn't hear of it. Mom
had told him that he didn't understand the problems of
child custody laws. And even when Emily tried to chime
in, Mom had shut her down. Mom said she didn't want to
hear a single word from either of them right then, that she
needed them to be quiet so she could focus on driving safely
and so she could figure out what their next move might be.

For the next hour, Emily wrote in her journal. She
wrote and wrote and wrote. And as she wrote, she remembered a book she'd just read. She'd picked it out just before
Christmas break from the recommended reading list from
her English class. Morgan had thought the book looked
boring, but the story had really gotten to Emily. In fact, she
wished she'd brought it with her because she thought she'd
like to read it again.

It was called *Anne Frank: The Diary of a Young Girl*.
The girl in the book, Anne, had been a real person. And,
like Emily, she had written in a diary about her life. And,
like Emily, Anne had been thirteen. And she had been
faced with a frightening dilemma. But Anne's troubles
were far worse than Emily's. And by the time Emily
finished the book, which in Emily's opinion was too short,
she decided that Anne Frank was one of the bravest
people she had ever read about. And for some reason this
gave Emily a bit of hope.

If Anne Frank could be brave when all looked hopeless, so could Emily. Besides, Emily reminded herself, she
had God. That was something that Anne had struggled
with a lot. Emily wanted to go back in time and tell Anne
that God really was real and that she should trust him
more. Maybe Anne did eventually ... before she died in
the concentration camp.

And that's when Emily really began to pray. She begged
God to turn this thing around ... and to get them safely
back to Boscoe Bay. She wanted to have as much faith as
Morgan and Grandma right now. But as their car kept
driving about sixty miles an hour due south, it wasn't easy.

"I'm sorry if I sounded grouchy," Mom said finally.
"It's just that I am really stressed over this. It wasn't what I
wanted either."

"But I don't see why we have to be the ones on the
run," said Kyle from the passenger seat in front. "Dad's

the one who messed up. He should be running … from the law."

"It has to do with taking you kids across the state line," Mom explained. "Your dad used to warn me that if I ever ran, if I ever took you guys out of Idaho, he would hire a lawyer and get full custody. Do you know what that means?"

"That we'd have to live with dad?" said Kyle.

"Yes," Mom said with a sigh. "I know I should've done it differently, but I felt so desperate at the time. I just wanted to get away. I saw the chance and I took it."

"And I'm glad you did, Mom," said Emily from the backseat. "It was the right thing to do."

"It seemed right," agreed Mom. "But according to the law, it was wrong."

"Do you know that for sure?" asked Kyle.

"I know that your dad is your parent, as much as I am," said Mom. "And that means he has the right to accuse me of kidnapping—"

"Kidnapping?" cried Emily. "That is perfectly ridiculous. You know that we wanted to come with you, Mom. We hated how Dad treated you. He should be in jail!"

"Yes, I know," said Mom. "But sometimes the law doesn't work like that."

"Well, then the law is wrong," said Kyle.

"As soon as we get settled," said Mom, "and as soon as I can afford it, I will contact a lawyer. I was about to do that back in Boscoe Bay. I even had the name of a guy in town … but then this happened. I just never really thought your father would find us. I don't even see how he did. Especially after we changed our last name. I switched cars … I thought I did everything I could."

"Do you think it was from those two times my friends and I were photographed and in the newspaper?" asked Emily in a weak voice.

"I don't know …"

"It's such a small paper," said Kyle. "I don't see how."

Even so, Emily felt guilty. She hated to think that their problems were all her fault. She should've been more careful. But after getting settled into Boscoe Bay, after making new friends, she probably had let her guard down. She should've known that Dad wouldn't give up that easily on his family. He was a stubborn and proud man, and she should've known that he would do whatever it took to find them.

Emily had always been afraid of her dad. He had never actually hit her, not like he hit her mother or Kyle, but he had yelled at her and carried on to the point where Emily felt it was likely she'd be next. She had even tried to talk to someone about it once. She had trusted Aunt Becky. But Aunt Becky, just like everyone else, couldn't believe that Emily's dad would ever do anything like that. No one could imagine the rages that he could go into when things didn't go his way. He managed to keep up an image of such a nice guy when he was out in public. In fact, that was one of the things that would set him off. He didn't want anyone to mess up his perfect image. And he couldn't stand it when anyone in his family, whether it was Kyle or Mom or Emily, did anything that he felt was "inappropriate behavior." Dad loved the phrase *inappropriate behavior*. He had a whole list of things that could fall into that category. Emily wrote them down in her journal.

* Being disrespectful of Dad
  (It was okay to be disrespectful of Mom as long as it wasn't in public.)

* Not having perfect manners
  (It reflected poorly on Dad.)

* Wearing unclean or wrinkled clothing
  (It reflected poorly on their family.)

* Using bad grammar
  (although Dad sometimes did without knowing it)

* Getting a bad grade or in trouble at school
  (Kyle got caught skipping in middle school, and you would've thought he'd murdered someone.)

* Being late, not doing your chores, not standing up straight ...

Emily knew she could make the list longer if she thought hard enough, but she was tired of thinking about Dad. She wasn't sure if she actually hated him — and she

knew that was probably wrong — but she did know that
she didn't want to see him again, and she didn't want to
remember how it had been living in the same house with
him. And even though they had nicer things and more
money then, Emily would never choose to go back to that
kind of life. She had never felt comfortable in her home.
And she had never wanted to have friends over. She had
seen Dad tear into Kyle in front of a friend once, and she
had never wanted that to happen to her. As a result, she
didn't have many close friends. For sure, she'd never had
anyone like Morgan to hang with. This was so unfair.

"Mom," said Emily in a timid voice. "I was just thinking about something that Morgan's grandma told me."

"What's that?"

"Well, she said that it might be safer for you — and for
us — to stay in Boscoe Bay."

"Why would it be safer? Can you imagine what would
happen if your dad found us?" Mom shook her head. "He
would probably show up with the police, accuse me of kidnapping you two ... and for all I know they would take you
away and throw me in jail. How would that be safer?"

"That's so wrong," said Kyle as he hit his fist into the
dashboard.

"Morgan's grandma said that we have a *community* in
Boscoe Bay. She said we have friends who will stand up
for us and help. We have our friends in Harbor View and

friends at church. She said that we would be safer there than out here on our own. I mean, think about it, Mom, what would we do if Dad found us out here on the road or staying at some motel? We wouldn't have anyone to turn to."

"I'm sure that sounds sensible to Morgan's grandma," said Mom. "But she does not know your father. She doesn't know what that man is capable of. He can be very convincing. I tried before to tell people what he did … don't you remember what happened after that?"

"But you still have those photos I took of you, don't you?" asked Kyle. "That's proof of Dad's abuse. And Boscoe Bay is different than where we lived before. The people there don't know Dad. But they do know us."

"That's right," agreed Emily. "We might have a chance back in Boscoe Bay."

"But what about the law?" asked Mom. "Sure, we might have friends and all that, but what happens when the law says that taking you kids away from your father was wrong? What happens when he has the legal right to take you back and to put me in jail? What then?"

The car got silent again. Emily wanted to ask Mom if she knew these things for certain, if she had really looked into it, or if she was just believing things that Dad had told her — things that he used to frighten her. Emily could remember other times when Dad would scare Mom into seeing things his way. He would use his power to hurt and control her — and sometimes it seemed that Mom wasn't really thinking straight. Was this turning into one of those times?

"I'm hungry," said Emily. "I didn't have any lunch and I—"

"I'm hungry too," said Kyle. "Can we stop and get something in the next town?"

"And I need to use a restroom," added Emily. But what she was thinking was she wanted to find a pay phone. She wanted to call Morgan's grandma and get some more advice.

"Okay, we'll find a fast-food place," said Mom. "And we'll order something to eat in the car. My plan is to drive until we get out of Oregon. Then we'll find a motel in some little town in northern California. But that's as far as I've planned so far."

After about twenty minutes they came to a town, and Mom drove until Kyle spotted a McDonald's. Emily told Mom what she wanted, and then pretending to go to the restroom, she went to the pay phone instead, placing a collect call to Morgan's house.

"Hello?" said Morgan's grandma.

"Grandma," said Emily happily, remembering how she had invited Emily to call her that the very first day they'd met.

"Oh, Emily, honey, how *are* you?"

"Okay, I guess."

"*Where* are you?"

Emily told her. Then she told her about her mom's plan about getting past the state line and staying in the first small town in California. "I'm not even sure where, exactly, but I'll try to call from there."

"Can't you ask your mother to come back?"

"I so wish!" Emily said quickly. "This is the deal, Grandma. My mom is so scared of my dad that she's just really freaked. And I don't think she's really thought this whole thing through, you know what I mean?"

"I understand, Emily … but you should know that your friend Chelsea was here a while ago," said Grandma. "And her father is contacting a lawyer friend — a Mr. Lawrence, I believe — and he may want to help your mom."

"I babysat for him," said Emily as she remembered earning money for the ski trip, the ski trip that she was going to miss now. "He's a nice guy."

"So, perhaps you should give Chelsea a call, dear."

"Okay. I'll do that."

"And, remember, we all want to help you and your family. Tell your mother she has good friends here, folks who will do what they can to help her. And tell her, Emily, that there must be a way to work this thing out without you poor kids always being on the run. God has better answers."

"I'll try to make her see that." Emily thanked Grandma now and hung up, immediately placing a collect call to Chelsea's cell phone and hoping that Chelsea would accept the charges.

"Emily!" cried Chelsea. "Is it really you?"

"Yeah, and I have to talk fast. Mom'll get mad if she finds out what I'm doing. I just talked to Morgan's grandma and she said that Mr. Lawrence might be able to—"

"Yes! He wants to help your mom, Emily. He's doing some legal research right now. Can you call back at my house in a little while?"

"I don't think so ... we have to keep driving. But when we stop for the night, at a motel, I'll try to call again. Can I call collect at your house?"

"Of course!"

"I gotta go," said Emily as she noticed her mom's car waiting past the drive-in window now.

"Take care," said Chelsea. "We're all here for you, Emily. We love you, and we're really praying for you."

"Thanks." Then Emily hung up and, without even using the restroom, she dashed back out to the car.

"That took a while," said Emily's mom.

"There was a line," said Emily. And that was true. There was a line. It was just that Emily had not been in the line. Of course, now that they were on the road again, she wished that she had been.

chapter four

"Thanks," said Morgan as Mr. Greeley handed over the key to Emily's house. "I sure do wish the Adams hadn't left like that ..."

"You and me both, Morgan." He shook his head sadly. "Just don't seem right."

"Well, my friends and I are doing everything we can to help them to come back to Boscoe Bay—back where they belong."

Mr. Greeley almost smiled now. "Well, if anyone can make something like that happen, I'd wager it would be you and your friends, Morgan."

"And God," said Morgan. "We need his help."

"You let me know if I can be of any help too. If there's anything I can do, you just let me know. I care about that little family."

"I know you do," said Morgan. She suddenly remembered how it had been Emily who had broken through to Mr. Greeley. It had been Emily who had solved the mystery of Mr. Greeley's estranged son and told him about it. Of course, he would have a special place for Emily in his heart. For that matter, so did Morgan. They had to get her back here!

"Well, I better get going," said Morgan. "Thanks again."

Then she took off running through the rain, trying not to get drenched before she got to Emily's house. Even though it wasn't yet five o'clock, it was dark out. And not a single light was on in the Adams' house. Morgan fumbled in the darkness, trying to get the key into the door as rain dripped down her back. Finally she got it unlocked, opened the door, went in, and turned on the lights, both inside and out. That was much better. Much friendlier. She could almost make herself believe that Emily and her family hadn't really left. Or that they would be home shortly.

She walked through the living room, wondering what it was she was really looking for. She knew she needed some sort of clue … something to show her where Emily and her family were headed, some way that Morgan and the rest of her friends could locate them and help them. The living room looked much the same as it had when Emily was still here. The same furnishings and things that Morgan's mom had loaned and given them were there, along with some of the things that Emily's mom had purchased later.

Morgan was somewhat surprised to see that the TV was still there, since Emily's mom had worked hard to save for and buy it. But then it was probably too bulky to put in their car, along with all their other belongings.

Maybe Morgan's mom could put it in their storage shed for them, to save for them when they came back ... if they came back.

Morgan swallowed against the lump that was growing in her throat. Maybe Emily wasn't coming back. Maybe Morgan was just on a wild goose chase right now. She walked around the abandoned house and tried to imagine what it would be like if Emily really was gone for good. Would someone else move into this house? Would Morgan ever hear from Emily again? What if that was it? Was this the end of their friendship?

"No," Morgan said out loud, and her voice echoed in the hallway that led toward the bedrooms. "That's not faith talking." Then she started to pray again. She prayed aloud, asking God to help her to find something in this house that might show her where Emily was and how to reach her. And, once again, she asked God to watch over Emily and her brother and mom. She asked him to work out a way to get them back here. "The sooner the better, dear God," she prayed. "By Christmas would be nice. Thank you. Amen."

Feeling a little more faithful, Morgan walked through the kitchen now. It too looked the same. She looked at the notepad, even picking it up and holding it on an angle to the light, hoping she might detect some important number or destination. But it looked like a grocery list: milk, eggs,

cereal, bread. Nothing that seemed to lead to anything.
She looked at the wall phone. It was the old-fashioned
kind with a curly cord that kept it attached. If it was like
the phone at Grandma's, the one Mom had picked out,
Morgan could check the caller ID to see who had called
recently. That could provide a good clue. But, as it was, she
felt clueless.

She walked down the hallway and peeked in Emily's
mom's room. It was messier than usual, with some odd
bits and pieces of clothing strewn about, as if someone had
packed very quickly. Not enough time to take everything.
What if she'd left something behind that she needed?
Morgan felt a little guilty for looking through a grown-
up's room. It almost seemed like trespassing. And so she
continued on. Kyle's room had the same messy look, as
if someone had packed recklessly, in a hurry. Morgan
pushed a couple of the opened drawers back in, picked up
a stray sock and laid it on the dresser, and even straightened his bedspread.

Morgan stood by the door, looking at his room. If
you didn't know what was up, all that had gone on today,
you might think that the Adams were still living here. All
the furnishings were in place. Sports posters still hung on
Kyle's wall. Even his football and skateboard were still in
the corner, like Kyle would be back any minute.

Finally, Morgan went to Emily's room. She held her
breath as she turned on the overhead light. Everything

looked almost exactly the same here as well. Emily's bed was neatly made, the colorful plush pillows that she and Morgan had sewn together were lined up along the top, each one in place, all except for the tiger-striped one. That was Emily's favorite and the softest one of the bunch. Hopefully she had that one with her. Morgan pulled open one of Emily's drawers. Empty. The closet was empty too. It seemed that Emily had taken more time to pack. Morgan remembered how little Emily had brought with her when she first moved to Boscoe Bay — literally the clothes on her back. Morgan remembered that day, back when they'd first become friends. Emily had been knocked from her bike by one of the bullies. She'd hurt her knee and torn her jeans. And, later, when Morgan and Emily got better acquainted, Emily confessed that the reason she'd cried wasn't because of her knee, but because she'd torn her jeans — her only jeans. That's when Morgan had mended them and then given her some of the clothes from her own closet, things she still liked, but had outgrown. Emily had been so appreciative. And that was the beginning of a great friendship. A friendship that Morgan wasn't ready to let go of. They needed Emily and her family back here. They needed to stay together!

Morgan picked up a thin paperback book from Emily's dresser. It was one of the books that had been on their recommended reading list in English class, but Morgan had assumed by the rather ordinary-looking cover that it must've been pretty boring. Just a plain black and white photo of a kind of weird-looking girl named Anne Frank. Morgan had actually been surprised when Emily had chosen this book, when it seemed there were so many others that looked far more interesting. But then Emily was really into books — a lot more than Morgan. And Emily often read poetry and old-fashioned books that Morgan had absolutely no interest in.

At least that's what Morgan had thought ... until Emily had told her about something she'd just read. Then the book and the characters would seem to come to life, and Morgan would suddenly wonder if she'd missed something. Right now she mostly missed her best friend.

She flipped over the well-worn paperback to read the blurb on the back. The title of the book was *Diary of a Young Girl,* and all that Morgan knew was that it had been written by a girl a long time ago. Back when World War II was going on. Still, Emily had been saying how good it was, and she had teasingly reminded Morgan, "You really shouldn't judge a book by the cover."

Now, as Morgan read the words on the back, she realized that, once again, Emily was probably right. This "boring-looking book" was the story of a thirteen-year-old girl who had hidden with her family in a small attic space to escape persecution from the Nazis during the war. Judging by the blurb, the evil Nazis probably wanted to kill this girl and her family.

Morgan opened the book to the middle, a little trick she'd learned back in grade school, and began to read. And what she read completely surprised her. She actually sat down on Emily's bed and continued to read several pages, getting totally caught up in Anne's story. This teenage girl described the sad conditions of living in a tiny attic with her relatives and not having enough food to eat and having to remain deathly quiet during the daytime. And yet this girl sounded so real and funny and smart. Morgan knew that she would have to read the whole book now, starting from the beginning. Then she and Emily could talk about it. That is if Emily got to come back.

Morgan was about to give up when she heard someone knocking. It sounded like the front door. It was probably Mom, home from work and coming to check on her. She'd probably seen the note Morgan had left on the kitchen table, saying she'd come over here to look around. Maybe Mom wanted to help. Or maybe Mom had some kind of news. Feeling suddenly hopeful, Morgan ran through the house to the front door and was just starting to unlock it when the knocking grew intense. It was more like banging than knocking. She paused with her hand frozen on the doorknob. And just then she heard a man's voice shouting loudly.

"Let me in, Lisa! I know you're in there!"

Morgan jerked her hand away from the doorknob, thankful that she had locked it behind her and that it was still locked. Then she stood on tiptoe to peer through the peephole. There, standing under the porch light, was a soggy and angry-faced man. He was swearing and beating on the door like he meant to break it down.

"I can hear you, Lisa!" He yelled. "I know you're there. You better open this door right this minute, or I'm going to kick it in."

With a pounding heart, Morgan slowly backed away from the door. Then she ran to the kitchen and grabbed the phone receiver, immediately dialing her own number, but then wishing she'd called 9-1-1 instead. Too late, Grandma had answered. Her calm, soothing voice seemed out of place with the furious sound of banging and yelling from the direction of the front door.

"Grandma!" said Morgan urgently. "I'm at Emily's house. Someone is trying to break in. Probably Emily's dad. Call the police *right now*. I gotta go!"

Then she hung up the phone, dashed down the hallway, and went straight for Emily's room because it felt the most familiar. But where could she hide? Knowing she couldn't hide beneath the futon bed, she headed for the closet and went inside. She was just closing the door behind her when she heard a loud crash coming from the living room. Morgan shuddered. Emily's dad had broken into the house! And right now, he was stomping through the living room!

Dear God, help me, she prayed silently.

chapter five

The rain finally let up, but it was pitch black out now, and Emily wished that Mom would drive a little slower. Still, she didn't want to say anything, didn't want to upset Mom any more than she already seemed to be. So Emily just prayed. She prayed and prayed and prayed. The car was silent, and Emily wondered if Kyle had actually fallen asleep. She wished she could fall asleep too. Maybe she would wake up and find out this had all been a bad dream. She also wished that she'd taken the time to use the restroom at McDonald's.

"I need a bathroom break," she finally said, interrupting the silence in the darkened car.

"I thought you went back at McDonald's."

"I can't help it if I have to go again," said Emily. "I think it was something in my cheeseburger."

Mom made a tired sigh. "Well, I suppose I could get gas in the next town. Can you wait that long?"

"I guess so."

"Or you can get out along the side of the road and—"

"No thanks," said Emily. "I can wait." Besides, she told herself, if Mom stopped at a gas station, there might be a pay phone she could use on her way to the bathroom.

But when they got to the next town, the bathrooms were off to the side and the pay phone was in obvious view of the car. There was no way Emily could use the phone without being seen by Mom. Unless …

"Don't you guys need to use the restroom too?" Emily asked when she returned to the car.

"You know, that's not a bad idea," said Mom. "It'll be at least three hours before we get to the motel. Kyle, maybe we should both use the facilities while we're here."

Then as they made their way to the restrooms, Emily made a fast break for the phone. But to her dismay, it was broken. The receiver was totally ripped off from the phone. "Why do people do things like this?" she said aloud as she walked back to the car.

"Hey, there's a pay phone in the office too," the gas guy called out to her.

"Thanks," she said. She considered running inside to use the phone, but felt too worried that Mom would be coming back and catch her and get mad. "I'm okay," she told him as she casually walked back to the car. What she really wanted to say was, "Help, I'm being held hostage by a crazy woman," but she knew that wasn't really true … or fair. She knew that most of all, Mom was just scared. And Emily also knew that Mom had good reason to be scared. If Dad did find them, he would take out most of his anger on Mom. And after that he'd take it out on Kyle. And, if he was mad enough, he might take the rest of it out on Emily.

The gas guy gave her a friendly nod and said, "Merry Christmas," before he went back inside to the dry office. He probably just assumed her family was off on a happy road trip, on their way to visit family for the holidays. If only that was the case.

Mom and Kyle returned and piled into the car. Soon they were back on the road again — a twisting, curving, dark, wet road that seemed to lead to nowhere, or worse. Emily kept imagining that they would meet their dad at the end of their travels. He'd be waiting for them in his big blue Ford Explorer. He'd make them all get out of the car, probably making arrangements to have it picked up and towed home, and then he would drive them back to Idaho. More than ever, Emily trusted Morgan's grandma's advice. They would be much better off back in Boscoe Bay!

"I still think this is totally crazy," Emily said to Mom.

"That's because you're a child." Mom's voice was getting more and more irritated sounding.

"I think it's crazy too," said Kyle.

"Well, lucky for you two, I'm the grown-up here, and I'm the one making the decisions for this family's welfare."

"But what about what Morgan's grandma said …" Emily tried to remember exactly what she'd been told.

"What would we do if Dad found us out on our own like this? We wouldn't have any friends or anyone to call for help. We don't even have a cell phone, Mom."

"That's right," said Kyle. "And if Dad ever does find us, you know he's going to be furious. Who knows what he might do?"

"That's exactly why we are making ourselves scarce. My plan is to become invisible."

"But how do you do that, Mom?" demanded Kyle.

"We'll go someplace where he won't find us. We'll change our names."

"But you said Dad wouldn't find us when we came to Boscoe Bay," persisted Kyle. "And you said by changing our names and living in such a small town, we would be safe."

"That's true," said Emily. "You did tell us that."

"Well, I'm sorry. I was wrong last time. But I won't be wrong this time. This time we won't just change our names, I'll change my social security number as well. I have a feeling that's what gave us away. And then we won't go for a small town this time. That was a mistake. We'll pick a large town. I think maybe somewhere in southern California … somewhere warm."

"But we won't have the kind of community that we had in Boscoe Bay," said Emily, remembering Grandma's points now. "We won't have the kinds of friends and neighbors that can be a support system. In a big city, we'll just be lost in the crowd."

"Exactly," said Mom. "That's the plan — to be lost in the crowd."

Emily sighed. Maybe that sounded like a good plan to Mom, but it sounded lousy to Emily. She would do anything to get Mom to turn this car around and go back home to Harbor View Mobile-Home Park. It was ironic too, because Emily remembered how she'd felt when they first moved there last spring. She thought the place looked pretty crummy. But then she and her friends had fixed it up. They had their clubhouse. And now it seemed more like home than ever.

"Why don't you turn on the radio, Kyle?" Mom suggested. "It might help us to get our minds off of ... other things."

But the drone of music didn't help Emily get her mind off of anything. All she could think was that they were making a big fat mistake. And the idea of Dad finding them out here with no one to stand up for them was truly frightening. Why couldn't Mom see that?

Emily leaned back into the seat, pulling the plush tiger-striped pillow toward her face. Morgan had helped her to sew this pillow, as well as several others for her bedroom. Then Emily remembered how they'd fixed up their clubhouse in the school bus, sewing pillows and curtains and all sorts of cool things. Tears filled Emily's eyes to think that she'd never get to go back to the clubhouse again. She would never go to another meeting, another party, or simply just a quiet escape to the bus. Worst of all, she would never see her friends again. Morgan, Carlie, Chelsea, and Amy were the best friends she'd ever had. And after a little more than six months, they were gone. It was so unfair.

She thought about the ski trip that she'd worked so hard to be able to go on, and how she'd actually gotten fairly good at snowboarding with Chelsea during Thanksgiving. And all for what?

Why are you doing this to me? she prayed silently. *God, I need you more than ever right now, and it feels like my whole life is just falling apart. Can't you do something? Can't you help me?* And, despite wanting to be brave like Anne Frank, the tears came pouring down. She pressed her face into the furry pillow to muffle the sound of her sobs. There seemed no point in upsetting Mom any more than she already was. Nothing was going to stop her from getting them far, far away. Life as Emily had known it was not only over and done with, it was out of control.

chapter six

Morgan hunkered down in the corner of Emily's darkened closet, curled into a tight little ball with her hands wrapped around her head as if that might somehow protect her from the evil force that was now prowling — make that stomping — through Emily's house. With what felt like a jackhammer pounding away in her chest, Morgan prayed desperately in silence. At least she hoped it was silent. Because what she really wanted to do right now was to yell and scream — and to cry out to God for help.

Morgan stared at the bright strip of light beneath the closed closet door. She wished she'd thought to turn off the overhead light in Emily's room. Hopefully that wouldn't lead the wild man directly to her hiding spot. But then she remembered that she'd left all the lights on throughout the house. Hopefully that would deter him for a while, long enough for Grandma to send help. And hopefully Grandma wouldn't come over here herself. She was under strict doctor's orders to remain at home, to remain calm. Suddenly Morgan was seriously worried about Grandma. And now she prayed for her. She prayed that Grandma would be sensible and not do anything to harm her health.

Then, for no explainable reason, she thought about what she'd read in that Anne Frank book just a few minutes ago. Somehow, it reminded her of how she felt right this very moment. Perhaps it was this hiding in a small space, the fear of being discovered. She felt helpless, almost less than human — like an animal being hunted. And, as silly as it seemed under her circumstances, she was more determined than ever that she would read that entire book — that is if she ever made it safely out of this closet. *Dear God, please help me,* she prayed urgently again. *Send help soon!*

"I know you're here!" His voice grew louder, as if he was closer now. Morgan guessed that he was in the hallway, probably going through the bedrooms. Maybe searching in the closets. Morgan curled even tighter into her ball, as if she might actually be able to vanish into the wall that was next to her.

"You might as well come out, Lisa! I've come for the kids, and I intend to take them with me tonight." Doors banged open and shut, and the crazy man kept yelling, stomping about, making threats, and using bad language. Morgan eased herself down onto her knees now as she tried to scoot more tightly into the corner, folding herself over into what was a praying position, which seemed entirely appropriate. She felt something spongy with her hand. She gently squeezed it, trying to determine what it was. Then she realized it was one of Emily's flip-flops, a pair that Morgan had given her last spring. For a distraction from the monster who was still yelling and slamming things around, Morgan tried to recall what color the rubber flip-flops were. It seemed like they were baby blue. Almost the same color as Emily's eyes or the summer sky. Morgan tried to imagine that exact color and happier times as the sound of Emily's dad's footsteps and yelling came closer and closer. She knew he was in Emily's room now. And, clinging to the flip-flop, Morgan continued to pray in silence.

"Aha!" His voice softened a little now, as if he was trying to sound like a nice person. "I'll bet that you're the one who's home, Emily. Where are you hiding, Baby Doll? Where's Daddy's little girl?" Morgan thought his voice sounded about as genuine as a three-dollar bill, and she felt sorrier than ever for poor Emily. What a beast of a dad!

"I know you're here, Emily. I could hear you running through the house. Come out, come out, wherever you are."

Morgan's heart was pounding so hard now that she felt certain that half the neighborhood must be able to hear it. She flattened herself down even tighter against the floor and into the corner, wishing more than ever that she could simply disappear. But the footsteps were coming directly to the closet, and then the metal doors squeaked open.

"So there you are, Emily," said the man. His voice grew stern again. "Why didn't you answer when I called you? It's time to quit playing games, little girl. I'm taking you all back with me. Come on, now, Emily. Don't make me have to yank you by the —"

Without even knowing what hit her, Morgan stood up and turned to face this horrible man, looking him straight in the eyes. "I am not Emily."

He sort of blinked, and then got a mean-looking smile. "No, you certainly are not. You're the wrong color." He swore. "It just figures Lisa would bring my kids to a trashy neighborhood like this."

Morgan took in a deep breath and considered trying to bolt past this horrible man, although it looked hopeless. Perhaps this was a good time to let out a big, long scream.

"What are you doing in my wife's house anyway?" He stepped closer. "Did you break in to steal something, you little —"

"Put your hands in the air!" yelled someone from behind Emily's dad. "NOW!"

Emily's dad slowly raised his hands above his head. And Morgan slowly released the breath that she had been holding, the one she was going to use to scream for help.

"Now turn around, nice and slow." Morgan recognized the voice now. She peeked out to see Mr. Greeley with a metal baseball bat held high in the air like a weapon.

The look on Mr. Greeley's face was dead serious and a little bit frightening, although Morgan realized he was here to help her.

"Who the—"

"Never mind who I am," yelled Mr. Greeley. "Just keep your hands in the air before I knock your stinking head off. Morgan, girl, you get down low. Get yourself back in the corner of that closet, just in case I need to start swinging this thing."

Morgan did exactly as she was told. And this time she didn't feel quite as frightened.

"Who do you think you are?" demanded Emily's dad.

"I was about to ask you the same thing," growled Mr. Greeley.

Then Emily's dad spoke in a somewhat calmer tone. "Look, Mister. I have a legal right to be here. This is my wife's house. And I've come to take her and my kids back home with me. The law's on my side."

"We'll see about that," barked Mr. Greeley. "In the meantime, you keep your hands up high and you walk nice and slow into the living room."

"But you can't just come in here and—"

"And shut your trap!" yelled Mr. Greeley. "Before I start swinging this thing."

"But you—"

"Move it!" snapped Greeley.

Morgan listened as their feet slowly walked down the hallway and away. Emily's dad was still trying to reason with Mr. Greeley, his voice seemed to be growing calmer and more persuasive. Almost to the point where Morgan herself might believe him — if she hadn't seen and heard what he was really like. She just hoped that Mr. Greeley wouldn't fall for that evil man's trickery. And she prayed that he'd keep that metal bat handy until the police arrived, which seemed like it should be happening any minute now. Morgan decided to count, hoping that by the time she reached sixty, the police would be here. But she had just said fourteen when she heard the sounds of sirens approaching their neighborhood. And before long she heard more voices and more footsteps. Still, Morgan was afraid to move. What if the police had to use their guns?

"You can come on out now, Morgan," called Mr. Greeley's voice.

Morgan slowly stood up, peering out of the closet to see Mr. Greeley standing there. But the baseball bat was gone. "Do the police have him now?" she asked warily.

Mr. Greeley nodded with a slight smile. "I hope I didn't scare you too much with my tough-guy talk."

"No way, Mr. Greeley. You were my hero!" Then she ran over and wrapped her arms around him in a tight hug. And to her surprise he hugged her back.

"I'm just glad you're okay," he said as they both stepped back.

Morgan's heart was still thudding like a marching band drum. She wasn't sure if it would ever stop pounding like that. "Thank you for rescuing me," she told him.

Mr. Greeley looked down at his feet. "Oh, it wasn't such a big deal. Just making sure you were safe."

"Morgan!" cried a frantic voice that sounded just like Mom.

"I'm in here," yelled Morgan, running straight for her Mom, grabbing onto her and holding tight.

"I was so worried!" cried Mom as she ran her hands over Morgan's hair then looked down and studied her face. "Are you really okay, Sweetie?"

"I'm fine, Mom. Everything's okay now."

"Grandma called me on my cell phone and told me what was happening. I was on my way home from work and driving as fast as I could, and then I got here and saw the police cars, and I was just so worried that—"

"Really, Mom," Morgan assured her. "I'm okay. Mr. Greeley came over here and saved me."

"Thank you so much, Mr. Greeley." Mom turned to him with tears in her eyes as she grasped his hand between both of hers. "I am so grateful that you were here. Thank you so much!"

He nodded shyly. "Just doing what needed to be done. That's all."

"But you should've seen him, Mom," said Morgan proudly. "He was just like some hero in a movie."

Mr. Greeley just waved his hand and said, "Nah, wasn't nothin' like that."

"Is that really Emily's dad in there?" asked Mom.

"I reckon so," said Mr. Greeley.

"It sure is," said Morgan with conviction. "I heard him talking and everything. He's a totally wicked man, Mom."

"The police said they'll be wanting to take our statements," Mr. Greeley told Morgan. "Are you up to talking to them now?"

"Sure am," said Morgan, standing straighter.

Morgan was relieved that Emily's dad had been removed from the house. Hopefully locked up for a long, long time.

"I'm Sergeant Moreno," said a policeman from the hallway. "I'd like to ask you some questions."

So the three of them sat on the couch while Sergeant Moreno began to ask Morgan and Mr. Greeley some basic things like their full names, addresses, and phone numbers. Morgan wished he'd hurry up to the important part. She was eager to tell her side of the story. But then he started with Mr. Greeley, asking what had made him come over to the Adams' house armed with a baseball bat.

"Well, I knew that Morgan was over here by herself," began Mr. Greeley. "But then I saw that strange car in the driveway. I knew that Lisa had run with the kids, and that she was in fear for her safety, saying that her ex-husband was dangerous. So I suspected it might be him over here, and I figured I might need a weapon with me. I didn't have time to call the cops."

"My grandma did," offered Morgan. "I called her when I thought something was up."

"That's right," said Mom. "My mother called me right after she called the police." Mom got a worried look. "In fact, if you'll excuse me, I'll give her a quick call to let her know all is well. She just had heart surgery."

Mr. Greeley answered a few more questions, and then Morgan got to tell the sergeant her side of the story, carefully giving him all the details.

"You have a good memory," Sergeant Moreno told Morgan. He turned to her mom. "Is your daughter always this descriptive?"

Mom smiled. "And you can trust her for giving it to you straight." She patted Morgan's hand. "I'm proud to say she is a very honest person."

"So, the intruder really said all those things?" the sergeant asked Morgan. "Made all those threats just like you said?"

Morgan nodded. "Except that I didn't use the swear words he used. I don't like to talk like that."

"Good for you."

"Mr. Adams is a very evil man," Morgan said finally. The sergeant frowned. "Mr. Adams?"

"You know … Emily's dad, the guy who broke in here."

"Oh …" He jotted something down in his notebook. "His name's not Adams. It's Chambers. Ken Chambers."

"That's right," said Mr. Greeley. "Lisa told me when they first moved here that she had to use a new name to protect herself and her family."

"So she and her children go by Adams now?"

"That's right," said Morgan.

"And where are they now?" asked the sergeant.

"We don't know for sure," said Morgan.

"Yes, we do," Mom said. "Or at least we know which way they're heading. My mother just told me that Emily called our house earlier. It must've been while Morgan was over here. It seems that she and her family were in West Port at the time. Emily called from a pay phone at the McDonald's there."

"So Grandma was right, they *were* going south," said Morgan.

"They're probably still on the road," Mom told them. "The plan, it seems, was to make it to the California border and spend the night in a motel before they headed on in the morning."

"I don't suppose you know the car's license number?" asked Sergeant Moreno.

"I can describe the car," offered Morgan.

"You know, I think I've got the license number over there in my office," said Mr. Greeley quickly. "I didn't even think about that earlier."

"That's great," said the sergeant. "We can put out an APB, and hopefully get that family back here so that Mrs. Chambers can press charges."

"And we have a lawyer all set to help her," said Morgan.

"You do?" Mom gave her a surprised look.

"Yeah, a friend of Chelsea's dad wants to help her."

"You girls didn't waste any time, did you?" Mom winked at Morgan.

"We had to work fast," said Morgan. "Emily's part of our club. She's like a sister. We need to keep her here so we can stick together."

Sergeant Moreno smiled. "Well, you people are fortunate to live in a neighborhood where folks keep an eye out for each other. This whole thing could've turned out so much worse."

Morgan and Mom described Emily's family and the car to him now, right down to the dent in the right front fender.

"That's great," said the sergeant as they were leaving. He paused by the broken-down door. "But what about this?" He said to Mr. Greeley. "Should I send someone over to put a —"

"It's under control," Mr. Greeley told him. "Got a brand new door out in my shop right now. I'll have it back up even before the Adams — I mean the Chambers — get back here."

"Because they are coming back here," said Morgan. "Right?"

"Don't see why not," said the sergeant as he closed hisnotebook. Then he thanked them and they went their separate ways.

chapter seven

The car was quiet now. There was just the sound of the tires hissing down the wet road, the thump-thump of the windshield wipers going back and forth, and the grainy hum of the car's radio. Kyle had tuned to a popular coastal station, which was slowly fading out as they continued driving south. Emily was about to try talking some sense to Mom again when she suddenly became aware of a different sound. Kind of a whining sound, like a mosquito, but not on a wet rainy night like this. She turned around in the backseat and peered back behind them to see flashing blue lights slowly getting closer.

"Hey, Mom," she said quickly. "There's a cop car behind us. With its lights on."

Kyle turned around in the front seat and looked back too. "Yeah, Mom, it looks like they're chasing someone. You better pull over and let them pass."

"I haven't seen anyone else on the road," said Mom as she turned on her signal and slowed down and pulled over.

Emily continued watching the cop car and its flashing blue lights. She expected it to zip right past them but, like them, it too slowed down and stopped directly behind their car.

"What?!" said Mom with an alarmed voice.

"Were you speeding?" asked Kyle.

"No, I don't think so."

"You were driving a little fast," pointed out Emily.

"But not enough —"

"The policeman is coming to the car," said Kyle.

"I know," growled Mom. "You guys better have your seatbelts on."

"We do," said Emily.

"It's probably nothing," said Kyle. "Maybe you have a taillight out."

Mom rolled down her window. "Is something wrong?" she asked the policeman who leaned down with a flashlight, pointing it into the interior of the car and shining it all around as if he expected to find something illegal going on.

"Are you Lisa Chambers?" he asked.

"Well, I … uh … I am Lisa Adams," Mom stammered.

"May I please see your license and registration, ma'am?"

Mom fumbled to find her purse, searching for her wallet. "I don't understand," she was saying. "I wasn't speeding, was I?"

The policeman just waited until she finally handed him the items he wanted. Then he stepped away from their car and returned to his own car.

"He called you Lisa Chambers," said Kyle in a voice that sounded as scared as Emily was starting to feel.

"That means he's talked to Dad," said Emily. Her stomach got a hard knot in it.

"Do you think Dad's with him?" asked Kyle.

Emily turned around to peer into the police car, but thanks to the bright flashing lights she couldn't see if anyone else was inside.

"I don't know," said Mom.

"What are we going to do?" asked Emily, truly frightened now.

"I don't know ..." Mom turned and looked back. "I could try to make a run for it."

"No," said Kyle. "That would be stupid."

Now Mom was starting to cry. "I *am* stupid," she said.

"No," said Emily in her firmest voice. "You're not stupid, Mom. Dad always tried to make you think that you were, but *you are not stupid*."

"Yeah, but leaving Boscoe Bay like this wasn't too smart," said Kyle.

"Kyle," said Emily in a warning voice. "That's not helping."

"He's coming back," said Kyle.

Mom rolled down her window again.

"Can you please step out of the car, ma'am?"

"But why?"

"I just need to talk to you," he said. "In private."

"Oh ... okay." Mom turned and looked helplessly at Emily and Kyle.

"We'll be fine," said Emily.

Then Mom got out, and she and the policeman went behind the car to speak. Emily wished she could read lips. But it was obvious when he used the name Chambers, that the policeman knew something about their family.

"I know that's Dad behind this," said Kyle in an angry voice. "He's probably in that cop car right now, just waiting to haul us back to Idaho."

A cold chill ran through her. "What will we do?"

"I'm not going with him."

"But what if the law's on his side, Kyle? What if he forces us to go home with him?"

"I'm gonna make a run for it, Emily."

"No, Kyle, don't do that. That's crazy. We're out in the middle of nowhere."

"I'll just head due west," said Kyle. "Straight for the beach. I'll find a place to spend—"

"No, Kyle! You can't do that."

"I can't go back with him."

"But it's cold out there, Kyle. And wet. And the police would be looking for you."

"I don't care."

"Kyle, please," she pleaded. "It'd just make things worse if you did that ... for you and everyone."

"Fine. You win. I'll stay." Then he swore.

"Kyle!"

"Sorry, Emily, but this just totally stinks. And I'll tell you what! I might go with Dad now, just cuz the cops are here. But I swear, the first chance I get, I'm gonna run for it. And I won't ever come back."

"Oh, Kyle!" Now Emily was crying again.

"Sorry, but I can't go back and live like that, Emily. Maybe it wasn't as bad for you. Dad always seemed to go a little easier on his Baby Doll."

"It was hard on me too, Kyle," sobbed Emily. "I don't want to go back either."

"Maybe you could run away with me."

"But how would we live? We're just kids, Kyle."

"Kids with parents who are totally nuts."

"At least one of them. You can't really blame Mom, Kyle. At least she was trying to get us away from him."

"Yeah, I guess she was right after all."

"Maybe so." Emily just shook her head.

"Dad's even got the law in Oregon in his back pocket. We don't have a chance against him."

"Yes, we do," said Emily suddenly.

"How's that?"

That's when Emily began to pray. Out loud this time. "Dear God," she prayed out loud, "Please, help us. We don't want to go back to live with Dad. He's a mean and wicked man. Please, please, help us out of this mess. I know you're my heavenly Father and that you love me more than any earthly father ever could. And I need you more than ever right now. We all do. Please, please, help us, dear God. Thank you. Amen."

"Like that's gonna change anything," said Kyle in a sarcastic tone.

"You don't know that."

"Yeah, right."

They sat silently in the car now. Emily turned around in the seat again, watching as the two figures stood in the drizzling rain, still talking.

"What can they possibly be saying for all this time?" demanded Emily impatiently.

"He's probably telling her that we have to go back with him." Kyle's voice was flat now, like he didn't care anymore, although Emily knew that he did. "The cop probably has some kind of court order from Dad. Maybe he's got a warrant for Mom's arrest. Dad probably accused her of kidnapping — that's a serious crime."

"Just like Mom said he would do." Emily kept watching. Now it seemed like Mom was the one asking the cop questions. And it almost looked like she was getting mad as she shook a fist at him.

"You better look, Kyle," she said quickly to her brother.

He turned around in his seat to watch. "Wow, Mom looks ticked."

"I'll say." Emily felt even more worried. "I hope she doesn't smack that cop."

"That would not be good."

"Hang on, Mom. Don't do anything stupid," Emily pleaded.

Despite Mom venting at the cop, she did not strike him, and he remained calm. Then, after she quit raging, his expression grew almost compassionate, and he actually placed a hand on Mom's shoulder, nodding and saying something that Emily assumed was supposed to be reassuring.

"Maybe he's telling her that their jail cells are clean," said Kyle in a cynical tone. "Saying that the beds aren't too uncomfortable, and that prison food is pretty good."

"Yeah, sure," said Emily, joining his pathetic game. "And he's probably telling her that her children will be perfectly safe in the custody of their father, and that as long as she cooperates, she has nothing to worry about."

"I just thought of something." Kyle's voice got serious now. "If we thought it was bad being with Dad before, can you imagine how bad it'll be if she's locked up and we're stuck with him without her?"

Emily could not imagine. And she almost wanted to tell Kyle that she'd changed her mind just now, and that making a run for it might be their best bet after all. Sleeping on the beach in the rain might be tough, but not as tough as going back to Dad without Mom.

Even so, she had a feeling that running away would be a mistake in the end ... and that it would backfire and they'd be in more trouble than ever. But she also had a strong feeling that this was the end of their little road trip. And suddenly she wasn't too sure she was ready for it to be over with now. She watched her mom's troubled face and felt guilty for the way she'd disagreed with Mom's escape plan right from the start. And she felt guilty for the way she'd slowed things down with phony bathroom breaks, which probably made it easier for the cops to find them. She also felt guilty for phoning her friends. For all Emily knew, that was how her dad had tracked them down. Emily felt worse than ever now.

If Mom went to jail, it would be partially due to Emily's interference. Perhaps Emily deserved getting stuck back with her dad. But her mom did not deserve getting stuck in jail. That was totally unfair!

chapter eight

"What a day you've had," said Mom as they walked away from Emily's house and back toward home.

"I'll say," said Morgan with a happy sigh. The rain had finally stopped and the Christmas lights on various houses in Harbor View made interesting reflections on the dark wet pavement. Morgan thought she'd like to paint something like this. It reminded her of a colorful beaded necklace against a piece of black velvet.

Mom ran her fingers through Morgan's curls as they crossed the street. "You still like your new hairdo?"

Morgan didn't answer. She didn't want to make Mom feel bad. She knew it had been expensive to have all her beaded braids removed a few weeks ago. But the truth was she really wished she'd never done it.

Mom paused on the porch. "You don't like it, do you?"

She looked up at Mom's bronze face, illuminated by the colorful Christmas lights on their house. Morgan kind of shrugged. "It's okay, I guess."

Mom started to smile. "Tell me the truth, Morgan."

"Okay, the truth is I did like the beaded braids better. I just didn't know it. I'm sorry, Mom. I know it was stupid to want to change my hair. I guess I thought it would make me more like my friends ... and then, after it was too late, I realized that I'd rather be more like me."

Mom threw back her head and laughed.

"That's funny?"

"No, Morgan, not funny like that. Just ironic, I suppose. Well, the truth is, I liked your beaded braids better too. In fact, I've been missing them."

"Me too," said Morgan as they went in the house.

"Well, if you want, you can get them back."

"Really?"

Mom nodded as she took off her coat and hung it on the hook by the door. "My treat, sweetie. I'll give Crystal a call this week."

Morgan hugged Mom. "Thank you! Thank you!"

"Hello there?" called Grandma from her recliner. "Is anyone going to fill me in on the rest of the story?"

"You go tell Grandma all the details of your latest adventure, and I'll start dinner," said Mom.

So, for the second time that night, Morgan retold the harrowing story of Mr. Chambers breaking into the house, her hiding in the closet, and Mr. Greeley's brave rescue.

"My goodness," said Grandma. "The good Lord was really watching out for you tonight, honey. I know I was praying my fool head off over here, stuck in this chair like this, but your mother gave me strict instructions not to set foot out of this house."

"And I'm glad you listened," called Mom from the kitchen.

"Well, I figured prayer was my best tool under the circumstances."

"Thanks for praying," said Morgan. "A lot of people have been praying today. And I can tell that it's made a difference. In fact, I should call my friends and tell them the good news. It looks like it's safe for Emily and her family to come back now."

Grandma nodded. "You go and call them, honey. I think I'll take a little nap before dinner. All this excitement has worn me out."

"Do you want me to help with dinner first?" Morgan asked Mom when she went into the kitchen.

"Call your friends," said Mom as she filled a pan with water. "Then you can help."

Morgan called Chelsea first, and for the third time tonight, she retold the story, slightly shortened this time.

"Wow," said Chelsea when she finished. "That's incredible."

"I know. It was a miracle."

"Well, I've sure been praying for one," said Chelsea. "I keep hoping that Emily will call me again."

"She called?"

"Yeah." Then Chelsea told Morgan about their quick conversation and how the lawyer was starting to research the case. "He really wants to help them."

"Well, he should call the police," said Morgan. "I'm sure they can fill him in a lot about Emily's dad and the charges against him already. Let me tell you, that guy is one scary dude."

"I'll let my dad know."

"Guess I better call the other girls. I know everyone has been seriously worried about Emily."

"Thanks, Morgan. Keep me posted."

"You too."

Next Morgan called Carlie, telling her an even shorter version of the still hard-to-believe story.

"No way!" shrieked Carlie.

"Way!" said Morgan, laughing.

"We wondered what was happening when we heard sirens in the mobile-home park. My dad went out to see, but since they were police cars, he wouldn't let us go out and look. I think he was afraid we'd get shot. I had no idea you were involved in that whole thing. I can't wait to tell my dad what was really coming down."

"Yeah, it was pretty weird."

"I'm sure glad I've been praying today."

"Yeah," said Morgan. "It's pretty much a miracle the way things are turning out. Anyway, I better call Amy now." So they said good-bye and Morgan tried Amy's house. When no one answered she tried the restaurant and got Amy on the second ring. She quickly retold the story once more. She was actually getting a tiny bit tired of it by now. Or maybe she was just tired in general.

"That's totally awesome," said Amy.

"Yeah," said Morgan. "I know ..."

"So, does this mean we'll still have our Christmas party at the clubhouse on Thursday?"

"Sure, we have some really great reasons to celebrate now."

"And Emily gets to go on the ski trip too?"

"I don't see why not."

"Cool."

"Yeah," said Morgan happily. "We are going to totally rock up there. I cannot wait!"

"Except for one thing," said Amy. "Uh, make that two."

"Huh?"

"Well, I ran into Jeff Sanders in town today."

"So?"

"So, he informed me that he and Enrico Valdez are both going on the ski trip."

"Why?" demanded Morgan. "They don't even go to our church."

"Well, neither do Carlie or I," Amy pointed out. "But I asked Jeff that exact same question, and it turns out that his uncle is your youth group leader, Cory What's-His-Name."

"No way. Cory is Jeff's uncle?"

"That's what he said."

"Well, that doesn't have to spoil anything for us," said Morgan with confidence. "Besides it's been a long time since those guys have bullied us, Amy. And they were actually pretty nice to us last summer. Remember the sandcastle contest?"

"And at least Derrick Smith won't be going," said Amy. "He's still in juvenile detention."

"So, we'll still have fun. A couple of boys can't ruin it for us."

"We'll have even more fun now that Emily is coming too. You know, Morgan, I was really praying hard for her today. I don't normally pray that much, but today I was asking God for a real miracle."

"It sounds like we all were, Amy. And it looks like that's just what we got."

"That is so cool — a real answer to prayer."

"Yeah. We have a lot to be thankful for." Morgan noticed Mom peeling potatoes. "But right now I need to go help make dinner."

"And I need to get back to work. It's starting to get busy here."

As Morgan hung up the phone, she decided it was time to ask God for something else. Emily and her family were still out there, still on the road and running for their lives. Morgan bowed her head and silently asked God to help the cops to find them, to turn them around, and to get them safely home. Then she went to help Mom in the kitchen.

"Do you think the cops will find the Adams — I mean the Chambers tonight?" asked Morgan as she peeled a potato.

"I hope so." Mom turned and adjusted the heat on the stove. "I know I wouldn't want to be in Lisa's shoes right now. She must feel so frightened … so alone."

"Maybe we could make them something tonight," said Morgan suddenly. "Something to put in their house to help make them feel welcome and at home again."

"Oh, Morgan, that's a super idea."

"But what should it be?"

"Well, I know Lisa felt bad that she hadn't had time to make any Christmas cookies. And since Grandma's surgery, she hasn't been able to do much in the kitchen either. Maybe you and I could give it a try — as long as we keep it simple."

"I'm sure Grandma will have some good suggestions," said Morgan.

As it turned out, Grandma had lots of ideas. And, after dinner, the three of them — Grandma coaching from her recliner — managed to put together all sorts of wonderful things, including microwave fudge, caramel corn, Russian teacakes, and candy-cane cookies. Morgan even made a big Welcome Home sign on the computer while the cookies were baking. Then she found a spare string of colored lights that she thought would look pretty hanging up around Emily's new front door.

Finally, they put all their goodies together to make two yummy-looking platters that even impressed Grandma.

"I know it's not as good as what you would do," said Morgan as she held one out in front of Grandma.

"I think it's wonderful." Grandma smacked her lips after taking a bite of fudge. "I may have to retire from the kitchen altogether."

"Please, don't," begged Morgan. "No one is as good a cook as you are."

Grandma smiled. "Well, I'm looking forward to getting back to it after the New Year."

"It's getting late," said Mom, pointing to the clock on the wall.

"Wow," said Morgan. "It's almost nine."

"If we want the Chambers to have these tonight, we should take them over right away."

"We'll need to get the key from Mr. Greeley again," said Morgan.

"That's right," said Mom as she wrapped plastic wrap over one of the trays.

Morgan peered out the kitchen window and across the street to see that the lights on his house were still on in his house. "I think we're in luck too. Looks like he's still awake."

"We better hurry," said Mom.

"Hey, we should take him something too, Mom."

"You're right, Morgan." Mom opened the cupboard and reached for another platter and in no time they had it loaded up for Mr. Greeley.

Then they put on their coats and headed across the street where Morgan happily presented Mr. Greeley with the platter. "We made it ourselves," she told him. "Just a small token of our appreciation for saving my life tonight." She had rehearsed that little speech in her head as they walked across the street to his house.

He grinned and thanked them both.

"And if you don't mind, we'd like to leave these platters at the Chambers' house," said Mom.

"Sort of a welcome home," added Morgan, glancing across the street to see that the driveway was still empty. But at least the porch light was on. "Do you think they'll get home tonight?"

Mr. Greeley frowned. "I don't rightly know, but I sure hope they get home soon — safe and sound, of course." He handed Morgan the key.

"We'll bring it right back," she promised. Then she and Mom headed across the street to Emily's house. Mom put the goodies on the kitchen table, and Morgan taped her sign on the archway that led to the kitchen. Then, together, they hung the lights around the front door.

"Did you check to make sure they work?" asked Mom as Morgan stooped down to plug them in.

"Presto!" said Morgan as the colorful lights came on.

"Lovely," said Mom. "Now let's get this key back to Mr. Greeley."

"This should be a nice welcome for them," said Morgan as they stood in the yard and admired the string of lights.

"I feel just like one of Santa's elves," said Mom as they hurried across the street again.

"It's going to be hard to go to sleep tonight," said Morgan after they returned the key. She glanced back at Emily's house. "Knowing that they're still out there … alone … maybe still scared …"

"Well, it should be a lot easier now that you know things are looking up for them," said Mom. "It's a much better scenario now than it was earlier today."

Morgan nodded. "Even so, I'm going to be praying extra hard until they get back."

"I think we all will be."

chapter nine

Just when Emily felt like she couldn't wait another second,
Mom finally came back and got into the car. But then
she just sat there in the driver's seat without speaking.
She stared straight ahead as if she'd just spent the last ten
minutes with aliens who had sucked every thought from
her head.

"Mom?" said Emily. "What's going on?"

Mom said nothing.

"Come on," demanded Kyle. "We need to know
what's up."

Mom slowly shook her head. "I'm not sure."

"Well, spill the beans, Mom," insisted Kyle. "What
did the cop say to you?"

"Yeah," said Emily. "We're pretty much freaking here."

"The policeman told me that your dad was in Boscoe
Bay."

"It figures," muttered Kyle.

"So he wasn't in the cop car?" asked Emily. At least
that was something.

"No ..." Mom shook her head again. "The policeman
said he's in jail."

"In jail?" exclaimed Kyle and Emily at the same time.

"No way," said Kyle skeptically.

"That was my reaction too, but the policeman said that it was true."

"Why?" asked Emily.

"Apparently, he broke into our house."

"That loser," said Kyle.

"And apparently it was fortunate that we weren't there."

"I guess so ..." said Emily, feeling slightly sick to her stomach now.

"But Morgan was there."

"Morgan?" Emily sat up straight in her seat. "Is she okay?"

"Yes, but apparently your dad threatened her."

"He threatened Morgan?" yelled Kyle. "I'd like to punch—"

"And then a man with a bat—"

"What?" demanded Kyle.

"The policeman said a neighbor, he said probably the manager—"

"Mr. Greeley!" yelled Emily.

"Yes," said Mom. "My guess too. Apparently Mr. Greeley showed up with a baseball bat and held your dad until the police arrived. Your dad's been charged with breaking and entering and, well, several other things too."

"That's fantastic," said Emily happily.

"Yeah," agreed Kyle. "I mean most kids wouldn't throw a party if their dad got arrested, but this is totally great."

"So the policeman wants us to turn around and drive back to Boscoe Bay now."

"Yeah!" said Emily.

"That's a five-hour drive," Mom pointed out. "We won't get back until midnight."

"That's okay," said Emily. "I don't mind staying up late."

"The policeman said we could stay in a motel if we were too tired to go back tonight," said Mom. "I don't know about you kids, but I feel exhausted."

"I can drive for you, Mom," offered Kyle. "I could use the practice, you know."

"So you kids really want to go back — back home — *tonight?*"

"Yeah!" they both cried at the same time.

Mom sighed and started the car. "I guess we can give it a try ... but no promises. It might be easier to just spend the night in the next motel and head for home in the morning."

"Whatever is best for you, Mom," said Emily. As badly as she wanted to be home tonight (right this minute in fact) she knew that Mom was probably as worn out emotionally as she was physically.

"Yeah," said Kyle. "You make the call, Mom. We won't complain."

"Well, let's get going and see how it goes."

"This is gonna be great, Mom," said Kyle hopefully. "We'll actually be *home* for Christmas."

"I hope so ..." Mom didn't sound completely convinced as she checked for traffic and then did a U-turn on the highway and started heading north. The police car did the same, following them — this time with the flashing blue lights turned off.

"And I need to tell you something else, Mom," said Emily. "I wasn't going to say anything until we stopped for the night and you could use a phone, but Chelsea's dad got you a lawyer. It's the guy I babysat for, Mr. Lawrence."

"And how did this happen?"

"Well, I guess Morgan told my friends about our situation. Chelsea called her dad and he set it up."

"See," said Kyle. "Morgan's grandma was right. It's better to take care of this kinda crud in a place where you've got friends to back you."

"I hope so," said Mom in a weary voice. "I really hope so ..."

After a couple of hours, Mom actually did allow Kyle to drive. Emily wasn't so sure about this since Kyle had only been driving for a few months now. But because it meant they didn't have to stay in a motel, and that they'd be sleeping in their own beds tonight, she didn't protest. But she did pray. And eventually she fell asleep.

"Wake up," said Mom as she nudged Emily. "We're home."

Emily sat up in the backseat and blinked into the darkness. "Home?"

"Yes." Mom tugged her by the hand. "It's one in the morning, but at least you'll be in your own bed soon. We can unpack our stuff in the morning."

"Look," said Emily, pointing to the Christmas lights around their door. "Santa has been here."

"Yeah, right," said Kyle as he grabbed his backpack.

"Hopefully that doesn't mean that someone else moved in here while we were gone," said Mom.

"Isn't the rent paid up to the end of the month?" said Kyle.

"Yes — oh, dear!" said Mom. "I don't have a key. I gave it to Mr. Greeley."

"Chill, Mom," said Kyle. "I still have mine."

So he let them in. And they were barely in the house when Emily noticed the Welcome Home sign. "Look, you guys!" she cried. "Someone is happy that we're back." She suspected, by the bright colors, that this was Morgan's work.

"And look here," called Kyle from the kitchen. "Someone brought us goodies."

"A party!" exclaimed Emily.

"Well, I suppose a few cookies and some milk before bed might help us to sleep," said Mom as she opened the fridge.

Soon they were all seated around the little table, munching sleepily on the treats that Emily suspected had come from the Evans' house, although she knew that Grandma was still restricted from the kitchen.

"It is nice to be home," said Mom with a happy sigh.

"And nice to have such good neighbors," added Emily.

"And nice to have our lives back," proclaimed Kyle.

Emily wanted to ask about Dad. So many questions were racing through her head. She wondered what would happen next — and what would they do if they let him out of jail? And what if Dad decided to stick around Boscoe Bay? How could they stop him from making their lives miserable? Would he try to force them to go back with him?

Still, she was determined not to ask these questions. Not yet anyway. The good thing was that they were home again — and they had good friends nearby. Somehow God was going to help them sort this whole thing out. And Emily felt certain that she'd be sleeping well tonight.

It was so great to be back in her room — to be around her own things and to sleep in her own bed. And before she got into bed, she got down on her knees and thanked God for doing a miracle today. She asked him to work out the rest of the details for her family. And then she got into bed and let out a long tired sigh and fell quickly to sleep.

Emily woke up fairly late in the morning. Still, it felt good to be in her own room and her own bed and not some stupid motel down in California. She got up and walked through her house, smiling happily to herself. Sometimes you just didn't know how good you had it until it was almost gone. It was good to be home! She went into the kitchen and was surprised to learn from Kyle that Mom had actually gone in to work today.

"She said figured she might as well earn some money," he told her as he poured a bowl of cereal for himself. "She said we're gonna need it now."

"Was she worried at all?" asked Emily. "I mean about Dad being around?"

He nodded as he poured milk. "Yeah, I think so. She warned me to stick around the house all day. She said to keep an eye on you and to call her or the police if anything developed."

"Meaning if Dad came here?"

"Yeah …"

"It is kinda scary, isn't it?"

Kyle shrugged. "It's not that big a deal. We can always call Mr. Greeley or the cops. And I doubt that the old man will be outta jail this soon anyway. Oh, yeah, Mom said for you to call Chelsea about that lawyer dude. Then call Mom at work and give her the lowdown. She wants legal help as soon as she can get it. That was the main reason she didn't want to miss work today. She said the attorney's fees would probably really set us back a ways."

"Well, it'll be worth it," said Emily as she filled a bowl with cereal.

"And it'll be cool to have our lives back ... and with our own real names again. That Adams-family thing might've been funny at first, but it was getting kinda old."

"Yeah," said Emily. "Dad might be a jerk, but I like the name Emily Chambers better than Emily Adams."

After breakfast, Emily called Morgan. "We're back," she said, suppressing a giggle.

"I know," said Morgan. "I got up early this morning and saw your car in the driveway. You cannot believe what good self-control I've had not to run over and knock on your door and give you a big welcome-home hug."

"Well, what's stopping you now?"

"I'm on my way," yelled Morgan.

Soon Morgan was sitting at the kitchen table with Kyle and Emily, relaying all the details of the previous evening.

"Wow," said Kyle. "Were you pretty scared?"

Morgan nodded. "Oh, yeah ..."

"Good thing Mr. Greeley was on top of things," said Emily. "I can just imagine him with a baseball bat wielded like a club."

"Yeah, making his grim Greeley face," added Kyle. "I'll bet that put the fear of something into our dad."

"It did at first," said Morgan. "But then your dad tried to talk Mr. Greeley out of it."

"That sounds about right."

"Fortunately, Mr. Greeley held his ground."

"I need to call Chelsea," said Emily, eager to end the conversation. The more she heard about her dad, the angrier she felt toward him.

"Yes," agreed Morgan. "I called her to tell her you were home. We knew you must've gotten in late, so we all agreed not to bug you so you could sleep in."

"It was close to two in the morning," said Emily as she went for the phone and dialed Chelsea's number.

"I'm so glad you're home," squealed Chelsea.

Emily asked about the lawyer, and Chelsea said he was eager to speak to her mom.

"Does he want to call her at work?" asked Emily. "It's okay. Mom really wants to talk to him."

"Sure, I can have Dad let him know."

"Uh, I think my mom's a little worried about how much this will cost. I mean we're not exactly —"

"It's pro bono," said Chelsea.

"Huh?" asked Emily.

"Pro bono."

"What does that mean?"

"It means Mr. Lawrence wants to do it for free."

"No way!"

"Yep. He does stuff like that sometimes, especially around Christmas."

"Wow."

"Well, I better let my dad know that your mom's at work," said Chelsea.

"And I'll let my mom know that Mr. Lawrence will be calling her."

"Hey," said Chelsea, "we should have a meeting today. We need to plan our Christmas party."

"Good idea," said Emily. "I'll check with Morgan and get back to you, okay?"

"Sounds good."

Then Emily called the Boscoe Bay Resort, but Mom wasn't available. So she left a voice message saying that Mr. Lawrence would be calling her. "And by the way, Mom," she added. "He'll be doing it *pro bono*." Then she said good-bye.

"Pro what?" asked Morgan after Emily hung up.

"Pro bono," said Emily as if everyone should know what that meant.

"You mean like Bono the guy from U2?" asked Kyle. "He's a pro."

"U-who?" asked Emily.

"U2."

"This is starting to sound like a knock-knock joke," laughed Morgan. "Who is pro bono?"

"Not who," said Emily, "what."

"Okay," said Kyle. "What is pro bono?"

"Pro bono means the lawyer, Mr. Lawrence, wants to take Mom's case for free. Pro bono means free."

"No way!" said Kyle.

"Yep." Emily grinned. "It really is good to be back here with our friends, isn't it?"

"You bet it is," said Morgan.

"Hey, thanks for the goodies," said Kyle as he popped a piece of fudge into his mouth.

"Yeah," said Emily. "That was really nice of you."

"Comin' home was sweet," said Kyle with a wink. "But that made it even sweeter."

"Chelsea thinks we should have a meeting," said Emily. "To plan the Christmas party."

"You're supposed to stay home today, Em," Kyle reminded her.

"You mean I can't go with my friends to the clubhouse?"

He seemed to consider this. "Well, I suppose if they're all with you and they escort you back and forth."

"Like my own special security guards?"

"Yeah." He nodded. "I guess it's okay. And Chelsea has a cell phone, doesn't she?"

"So does Amy," pointed out Morgan.

Soon it was settled. The girls would have an official meeting at two.

"In the meantime," said Kyle, "you can help me put all our stuff away."

"You mean that giant heap by the front door?" asked Morgan.

"Yeah. I helped Mom unload the car before she went to work. It looks like it's gonna take all day to get everything put away." He shook his head. "I can't believe what we almost did."

Emily couldn't either. But the best part about it was that it seemed to be over. Still, it was disturbing to know that her dad was in town, and that he knew where they lived. But she tried not to think of that as they began to put things away.

chapter ten

With Morgan's help, Kyle and Emily got almost everything, including most of Mom's stuff, back into place by one o'clock. Then, as they were standing in Emily's bedroom, Morgan picked up the Anne Frank book from off her dresser.

"Are you done with this?" she asked Emily.

"Yeah. I read it in like two days."

"Can I borrow it?"

Emily tried not to look too surprised. "Sure, what makes you think you'd like it?"

"Like you said, Em, you can't judge a book by the cover." Then Morgan explained how she'd read a few pages and got hooked. "In fact, I was thinking about Anne Frank when I was hiding in your closet last night."

"Yeah, I can understand that. She was in hiding for years."

"Anyway, I can't wait to read it."

"Cool," said Emily. "And then we'll talk about it, like a mini book club."

"It's a deal." Morgan gave her a high five.

"Now, I'm starving," said Emily.

"Hey, why don't you guys come over to my house for lunch?" suggested Morgan. "We've got some really good leftovers that I can warm up for you. And I know Grandma will be happy to see you."

After a hearty lunch, Kyle entrusted Emily over to the friends who had gathered at Morgan's house. "I guess you're in good hands now," he said to her. "Just be careful and call me if you … well, you know …"

"And you be sure and lock the door at home," she quietly told him.

Then her friends escorted her to the clubhouse. They made jokes and pretended to be secret-service agents, but a small part of Emily knew that this was not completely a joke. It was still fairly serious business. But once they were locked inside the bus, Emily felt safer than ever.

"Man, is it good to be home!" she said happily.

"I brought treats," said Chelsea, opening up her back-pack to produce some chips and soda. "Not the healthiest stuff, but I figured we had reason to celebrate."

For the next hour, the girls visited and laughed and enjoyed being back together again. Emily was relieved that they didn't spend too much time talking about her dad's unexpected appearance in Boscoe Bay. Her friends seemed to pretty much accept that he was a jerk and that it was in everyone's best interest that he was now in jail.

"I have an uncle who's in jail," admitted Carlie. "I didn't even know it, but when I told my dad about what happened with your dad, he told me about his older brother down in LA. I guess it was a similar situation. He'd been abusing his wife for years, and she finally pressed charges against him and he got locked up. My dad said it was a good thing."

Emily nodded. "Yeah, nobody should have to put up with that."

"Okay," said Amy, clapping her hands to get their attention. "We need to remember why we're having this meeting today." Then she reminded them that they were supposed to be planning for their much-anticipated Christmas party. The original idea, she pointed out, had been to dress up and invite family and friends from the mobile-home park and make it a really big deal.

"But what about this weather?" said Morgan, pointing out the window where the rain had just started to come down in buckets again. "Can you imagine everyone trekking out here to the bus and getting soaking wet in their nice party clothes?"

"You know, that party we had last summer was amazing," said Carlie. "But don't forget there were a lot of people here, and there was no way they could all be inside the bus at the same time."

"Yeah," said Morgan. "It was so warm that we had the party at the beach."

"Being outside of the bus on a rainy December night is not very appealing," said Chelsea.

"Not at all," said Amy. "And with everyone inside, it could get pretty crowded and stuffy."

"And I doubt the weather will cooperate," said Morgan. "This is, you know, the Oregon coast. Besides, do we really want everyone to know about our clubhouse?"

They briefly considered having their party in a different location, but that seemed to spoil everything. The point of the party was to be in the bus.

"I make a motion that we limit the party to just the five of us," said Amy finally.

"I second it," said Chelsea.

"And we can do our gift exchange," said Morgan.

"And we can decorate our Christmas tree," said Carlie with a sly grin.

"What Christmas tree?" asked Amy.

"I got a little one for the bus when I went out in the woods with my dad. I was saving it for the party."

So it was happily agreed — they would have their party on Thursday, just two days before Christmas.

"Hey, did you guys hear the news?" asked Amy. "About the ski trip?"

"You mean that Emily is going after all?" teased Carlie.

"No, I mean that our old enemies Jeff Sanders and Enrico Valdez are going."

"Why?" demanded Carlie.

So Amy explained, and Morgan tried to reassure everyone that it would be perfectly fine. "It's not like they'll be the only boys there," said Morgan. "And it's kind of cool that Jeff Sanders is Cory's nephew. I had no idea."

"And I think he's kind of cute," said Chelsea.

Emily wrinkled up her nose. "No way."

"Uh-huh," said Chelsea. "And he's nice too."

"Gross," said Emily, making an even worse face this time.

Chelsea poked Emily. "And I think you protest too much, Em. You know that Jeff likes you."

"Does not," said Emily. "Take it back."

"Chelsea's right," said Morgan. "Everyone knows that Jeff likes you, Emily. He's liked you ever since you moved here."

"Yeah, right, that day he and his bully friends knocked me off my bike. If that ain't love, I don't know what is."

They all laughed.

"You know," said Amy. "We really ought to be thankful for those boys."

"Why?" demanded Emily, still embarrassed by what Chelsea had just said about Jeff liking her. Okay, maybe he did like her, but Chelsea didn't have to go shooting her mouth off about it in front of everyone!

"Those stupid bullies were what originally got us girls together," proclaimed Amy. "It was their meanness that united us as friends."

"That's true," said Carlie. "And, to be fair, Enrico has been really nice to me this year. One day, right after school started, Andrea Benson bumped into me — on purpose I'm pretty sure — and I dropped my books all over the hallway floor, and Enrico stopped and helped me pick them up. I mean it was kinda embarrassing at first, having a boy helping me like that, and naturally Andrea made some totally lame comment, but it was kinda sweet too."

"Well, fortunately, Derrick Smith won't be on the ski trip," Amy informed them. "He's still locked up in juvie."

"You know, I feel sorry for him," admitted Emily. "He must be one pretty miserable kid."

"He sure likes making everyone else miserable too," said Carlie.

"You know what they say," said Morgan. "Misery loves company."

They laughed. But Emily couldn't help but feel sorry for poor Derrick. He was locked up and practically friendless. In a way, not unlike her own dad. Although she didn't feel sorry for her dad. She didn't care if he rotted in jail. And that thought alone made her want to think about something else.

"Well," said Emily. "I love being with you guys. And I am so totally jazzed to be home again. I've decided that it's true, you really don't know what you've got until someone tries to take it away."

"That's how we felt about you too," said Amy. "Suddenly you were gone, and it hadn't even been for a day and we really missed you."

Emily held up her soda can. "Here's to staying together!"

"To staying together," the others echoed.

chapter eleven

After Emily's friends escorted her home from their meeting, Chelsea asked if she could wait at Emily's house for her mom to pick her up.

"Sure," said Emily. "Unless you're afraid that my weirdo dad will show up and do something totally nutso." Emily tried to make this sound like a joke, but the truth was she felt a little uneasy. Just knowing her dad was in their town, that he had actually been in her house — even in Emily's own bedroom — was pretty upsetting. Creepy even. And, more than ever, Emily felt like she hated him. Not that it was a good feeling. It was not. But it was the truth.

"Nah," said Chelsea. "I'm not afraid. Besides my mom'll be here in a few minutes anyway."

"Any news?" Emily asked Kyle when they went inside.

He looked up from the video game he was playing. "Nope. All's quiet on the western front."

"Quiet is good," said Emily.

"Oh, by the way," said Chelsea. "My mom said to invite you guys to dinner tonight. She's going to call your mom at the resort to work it out. And the Lawrences are coming too."

"Cool," said Emily.

"My mom probably already gave your mom the details."

"Great."

"And while the grown-ups are talking, you and I can work on our wardrobe for the ski trip," said Chelsea. "It's not too soon to figure it out. The snowboarding pants I ordered arrived, and I can't wait for you to see them."

Emily nodded. "Sounds good." But what Emily was thinking was that she'd rather do that kind of planning with Morgan. Or at least include her. Still, she didn't think it would be proper to invite Morgan to Chelsea's tonight. And she didn't want to seem ungrateful to Chelsea for all the help her dad was getting for her family. Emily decided she'd just have to figure that out later. In the meantime, she felt certain that Morgan would understand.

"Chelsea, your mom's here," called Kyle from the living room.

"See ya tonight," said Chelsea as she grabbed her bag and left.

"So, I guess that means I have to go too," said Kyle after Chelsea was gone.

"You probably don't *have* to," said Emily. "But I don't see why you wouldn't want to. Besides, do you really want to be home alone … you know, when dad is in town?"

He frowned.

"Besides, the Landers are pretty nice."

"Don't you mean pretty rich?" Kyle sighed as if giving in. "I guess I wouldn't mind checking out their crib. I've only seen that place from the driveway."

"They have a billiards room," said Emily. "And pinball machines and everything."

"Okay," said Kyle a little more cheerfully. "Works for me."

Emily returned to putting her room back together … more carefully now. She checked out her closet for things she could take on the ski trip, but other than the Tommy Hilfiger outfit that Chelsea had given her, it was slim pickings. She had a feeling Chelsea would be in for a disappointment when it came to Emily's ability at any serious "wardrobe planning." Then Emily tried on the brightly colored polar fleece hat that Morgan had given to her as an early Christmas present. It was lively and cute, but she had a feeling Chelsea might not approve since it didn't have a designer label. But at the same time Emily was pretty sure that she didn't even care. Money, except when you really needed it for things like food or rent, was highly overrated.

When Mom got home, Emily was pleasantly surprised to see she was in a cheerful mood. She was actually humming a Christmas song as she hung up her coat. "Did you kids have a good day?"

"Yeah," said Emily. "Really good."

"And it was nice having the day off from work," said Kyle. "And luckily I still have my job at the station. The boss was pretty understanding. But he expects me to be there tomorrow for holiday traffic."

"We've been invited to dinner," announced Mom.

"We already know," said Emily. "Chelsea was here."

"So you'll be ready to go in about twenty minutes or so?"

"No problem," said Emily. She'd already changed into what she thought was an acceptable outfit of her best jeans and a sweater. Most of the times she'd been at Chelsea's had been pretty casual.

"And?" said Kyle impatiently. "Did you hear anything about Dad today, Mom?"

Mom smiled. "Yes. He's still in jail. Mr. Lawrence has already filed a restraining order on our behalf. It's looking really good."

Emily sighed in relief. "Aren't you glad we came back to Boscoe Bay?"

Mom nodded. "Yes. But I was in such a state yesterday, I just could not think straight. And, for the life of me, I could not imagine how this whole thing could possibly be resolved. But now I feel hopeful. After a brief conversation with the attorney, I think it might actually be achievable."

"And did you hear that he is doing the work …" Emily tried to remember the terminology. *"Pro bono?"*

"Yes, I could hardly believe it."

"We're gonna get through this," said Kyle.

"Absolutely," said Mom. "Now let's get ready to go. Kyle, can you put on a clean pair of pants?"

Kyle may have had on clean pants, and Emily had even worn a designer sweater that Chelsea had given her, and Mom looked nice, still wearing a dark pantsuit from work, but just the same, Emily felt like their family was out of place as they sat around the Landers' dinner table. She tried not to think about it too hard, and she hoped her mother didn't notice anything, but she felt uncomfortable.

It was weird, because she'd eaten at Chelsea's house lots of times, but it had never been like this. Tonight felt formal. Dinner was "served" in the fancy dining room with fancy dishes and crystal and silver and candles. Mr. Landers and Mr. Lawrence — both still dressed from work — had on business suits, Mrs. Landers had on a pretty red pantsuit, and even Chelsea was dressed a bit more nicely than she had been earlier today.

Not that this was just about the clothes … although Emily knew that her family looked shabby and poor next to these wealthy people. But it felt as if something more was happening here. The more the grown-ups talked about her family's troubles and how Mr. Lawrence would be helping them, the more Emily felt like her family did not belong here — not socially anyway — and the more she felt like her family was really just a charity case. A Christmas project to make the others feel good. And Emily hated feeling that way. It was so ungrateful … and judgmental.

"Can we be excused?" asked Chelsea after dessert was mostly finished. "We need to make some plans for our upcoming ski trip."

"You mean wardrobe plans," teased her mom.

"Of course," said Mr. Landers. "I'm sure this conversation must be boring to you kids."

Emily tried not to sigh in relief. She considered asking Kyle to join them, but she wasn't sure if Chelsea would be okay with that. Fortunately, Mr. Landers offered Kyle the use of the game room, and her brother seemed happy to make an escape too.

Once safely in Chelsea's room, Emily flopped into a chair. "Whew," she said. "Glad that's over."

"I know," said Chelsea. "Grown-ups can go on and on about the most boring details." She opened up her closet and started tossing out items of winter clothing. "I thought you could borrow some stuff for the ski trip," she said. "You know, like you did for the Thanksgiving trip."

"Oh, that's okay."

"Huh?" Chelsea turned and looked at her. "What do you mean?"

"I mean, that's okay. I don't need to borrow anything."

"Don't you wanna look hot up there?"

Emily shrugged. "I don't know ..."

"Are you feeling okay?" Chelsea came over and actually put her hand on Emily's forehead as if to see if she was running a temperature.

Emily forced a laugh and pushed her hand away. "I'm not sick."

"But something's wrong." Chelsea studied her face closely. "What?"

"I think I'm just kinda tired and overwhelmed from everything." Emily knew that was partially true, but she also knew that wasn't the total problem just now. Still, she wasn't sure she wanted to say what it was that was bugging her. Maybe it was really just her imagination.

"I'm sorry," said Chelsea. "I guess I'm not being very understanding. I just figured there wasn't much time, and we should plan what we're going to wear —"

"You know what I'd like to do?" said Emily, sitting up suddenly.

"What?"

"I'd like to plan what we're going to wear with all the girls in the club."

"Hey, that's a great idea."

"Yeah. Because most of us don't really have ski clothes. I mean who needs them unless you go up there a lot. So maybe we could sort of pool our things together and share stuff and have a packing party or something."

"That sounds like fun." Chelsea tossed her clothes back into her closet, not even bothering to hang them up. Of course, they had a housekeeper who took care of that.

"Maybe right after Christmas," suggested Emily.

"We can have it here if you think that's okay." Now Chelsea frowned. "I know, I probably come on too strong sometimes. But you know how I am about fashion."

Emily smiled. "Yeah, you really get into it."

"You got that right." She grabbed a magazine. "Hey, look at this pair of jeans. They are so cool."

So Emily humored Chelsea for a while, poring over her latest fashion rags and acting interested, until she finally she got so bored that she asked if they could go play a game of pool with Kyle.

"Okay," said Chelsea as she tossed a magazine aside. "That actually sounds like fun."

"I'm sure Kyle will appreciate some company … even if it is just us."

"You know, Kyle is getting to be really good-looking."

Emily rolled her eyes at her. "Puh-leeze."

Chelsea laughed. "Well, he is, Em. His skin is all cleared up now, and he got taller, and I can't help it if I noticed that he's looking really —"

"Fine, fine," said Emily quickly. "You think my brother is a hottee. Now let's not talk about it anymore. Eeuw."

But as they went downstairs, Emily wondered if Chelsea wasn't just starting to get a little too boy crazy. That was the second time today that she'd gone on about boys.

"Hey, Kyle," said Chelsea as they went into the game room. "We chicks wanna challenge you to a game of pool. You in?"

"You're on," said Kyle, picking up a cue.

Chelsea put some songs into the jukebox, and Emily helped Kyle to get the balls set up. She wondered if Kyle would be surprised to see that her pool skills had improved a bit since hanging with Chelsea. They'd played quite a few games down here in the past several weeks.

But the more the three of them played, the more irritated Emily felt at Chelsea. It was like she was actually flirting with Kyle. And it made Emily feel very uncomfortable. For one thing, Chelsea was only thirteen — three years younger than Kyle! For another thing, Kyle seemed to be enjoying the extra attention. But in Emily's opinion, Chelsea was acting like a total idiot. Emily was getting downright disgusted with both of them. Thankfully, Mom broke things up.

"Hey, kids," she called from the top of the stairs. "I hate to spoil the party, but it's been a long day for me, and I have to work tomorrow."

"That's okay," said Emily, perhaps a little too eagerly, as she put away her pool cue.

"Let me put this last one away," said Kyle, pocketing the eight ball in the corner pocket.

"You are such a good shot," said Chelsea.

Kyle grinned. "Thanks. And thanks for the games."

"Well, thanks for cleaning our clocks," said Chelsea, gently punching him in the arm.

"Anytime," said Kyle.

It was all Emily could do not to roll her eyes and groan. "Thanks for everything, Chelsea," she said instead. "See ya."

chapter twelve

The next day, Emily couldn't wait to get to Morgan's house. The plan was to work on the Christmas presents they'd been making for the other girls. And it felt so good to hang with Morgan and just be a regular kid again, creating things that would be fun to give to her friends. Whether it was beading or knitting or sewing, Emily just focused her attention on each project and enjoyed hanging with Morgan.

"This is so great," Emily said as they took a break to make themselves and Grandma some lunch. "I can't believe I almost lost all this."

"Me neither," said Morgan as she poured the second can of chicken and rice soup into the pan. "So, how's it going ... I mean with your dad and everything?"

Emily could tell that Morgan was still a little uncomfortable with all this. For that matter, so was Emily. Still, she'd been fairly honest with Morgan. She'd told her that — although she was relieved that her dad was locked up — it was still hard knowing that he was in town. She hadn't told Morgan that she hated him. As a Christian,

Emily knew she wasn't supposed to hate anyone. Even her enemies. She also knew that there was a commandment that said kids were supposed to respect their parents. This one really confused her. How was she supposed to respect someone like Dad?

"My mom is feeling pretty hopeful that the lawyer is going to get it all straightened out before long."

"No chance of your dad getting out of jail?"

"Not according to the lawyer. He said that bail is set pretty high, and it doesn't look like anyone is jumping in to help him out. Sounds like he'll be in there a while."

"How do you feel about that?" Morgan's forehead creased as she stirred the soup. "I mean, I realize he is your dad. Does it bother you knowing he's locked up?"

"It would bother me more if he wasn't." Emily laid a slice of cheddar cheese on top of a piece of bread.

Morgan nodded. "Me too."

"But the lawyer has already got a restraining order made out."

"That's good."

"So, even if he did get out, he would be in serious trouble if he came near any of us."

"You guys should probably get cell phones," said Morgan.

"Yeah … Mom's thinking the same thing."

"I wish my mom was thinking that too." Morgan laughed. "I keep hinting that a cell phone would be a good

Christmas present. But so far, I don't think she's buying it."

"Well, if we do get cell phones, my mom made it perfectly clear they will be those cheap ones, the kind that are only for emergency use."

"At least we have friends that have them." Morgan put one of the cheese sandwiches onto the hot grill, and they both watched it sizzling.

"Speaking of rich friends …" began Emily. "My mom and Kyle and I had dinner at the Landers, last night." She sliced another piece of cheese and handed it to Morgan, who was now putting the sandwiches together.

"Really?"

"Yeah. Mainly so that Mom could meet the lawyer and they could talk and stuff. But it was this really formal dinner with lots of silverware and glasses, and I felt like a fish outta water. I think Kyle did too. Of course, he didn't admit it."

Morgan laughed as she set the next sandwich on the grill. "Yeah, I just do not get why some people want to make something as simple as eating food so complicated."

Then, without even thinking, Emily began making fun of the Landers and all their fancy forks and things, but then she felt bad. After all, Chelsea's family was really helping hers.

"Sorry," said Emily. "I don't think that was very nice."

Morgan nodded. "I understand."

"I don't want to seem ungrateful … I just don't really want to feel like I owe them something too. You know?"

"You don't owe them a thing, Emily." Morgan pushed her glasses back up her nose and then shook her finger at her. "You shouldn't think that way. Just because one person helps another person doesn't mean that anyone owes anyone anything. Not if you're doing it for the right reasons anyway." She turned and gave the soup a stir.

"I'd like to believe that," said Emily.

"Well, then you better."

Then Emily told Morgan about the packing party that Chelsea wanted to have at her house before the ski trip.

"Why?" said Morgan as she flipped one of the grilled-cheese sandwiches.

"Well, I guess it was kinda my fault," admitted Emily. "Chelsea was trying to share some of her ski clothes and stuff with me — because she wants me to look all cool and fashionable when we go on the ski trip — and it sort of hurt my feelings, although I didn't let her know. And now that I think about it, I was probably pretty ungrateful about that too. I mean I shouldn't have been offended by her generosity."

"Oh, I don't know …"

"Anyway, I suggested that we could all get together, you know, since most of us don't have ski clothes or much snow stuff. I thought we could all share and plan our outfits together."

"Oh, I get it," said Morgan. "I guess that's a nice idea. And Carlie and Amy will probably appreciate it too."

"Poor Amy," said Emily. "She's so much smaller than the rest of us, she probably won't find anything she can use."

"Hats and scarves," said Morgan. "And I actually have several of those."

"Well, I guess it might be fun."

"You bet it'll be fun," said Morgan.

"Maybe we should do it at the clubhouse instead of Chelsea's," suggested Emily. "That way it might not feel as much about money and things as just having a good time."

"That's a great idea!"

So, after lunch, they called their friends and arranged to have everyone meet at the bus on the day after Christmas. Chelsea wasn't sure it was such a good idea, but Emily finally convinced her it would be fun, saying they could do fashion walks down the middle aisle of the bus, and pretend that they were on a fashion shoot.

"Hey, I'll bring my digital camera," said Chelsea, now fully on board.

"And don't forget that Amy is tiny," said Emily. "If you have any old things, you know, ski stuff that you've outgrown, bring them for her."

Then Emily and Morgan spent the rest of the day working on Christmas presents, listening to music, and just hanging. In fact, that's how Emily spent the next two days.

Then on Thursday, the girls got together at the clubhouse for their Christmas party and gift exchange. Morgan and Emily got there early, putting on some Christmas music and turning on the strings of lights. Then they set out the Christmas cookies that they'd made and frosted just yesterday. Then the others arrived, and Carlie set up the little Christmas tree in the driver's seat, and they decorated it with ornaments from home.

After that, they took turns opening their Christmas presents, starting with the ones from Morgan. She'd made each of the girls a brightly colored pair of polar fleece socks and matching hats.

"You might want these for the ski trip," she told them as they tried them on. Then Emily gave her friends the handmade beaded chokers that Morgan had helped her to make. Each one came with its own little drawstring bag, which Emily had sewn on Morgan's sewing machine. She had specially designed each necklace with each friend in mind. Everyone seemed to really like them, which made Emily feel good.

Carlie gave them all hand-painted ceramic dishes, which she explained she had decorated herself at the local pottery shop, personalizing each one with the girls' names before they were fired in the kiln. "You can use these to put your jewelry and things in," she told them happily.

After that, Amy gave them each a "free lunch" gift certificate for her family's restaurant, along with a bag of fortune cookies. "Okay, I guess I'm not as clever as you guys, because I didn't exactly make these myself," she admitted. "But it was the best I could do under the circumstances. We have been busier than ever this past week." She glanced at her watch. "In fact, don't let me forget that I have to get back there by four."

"Well, I didn't make my gifts either," said Chelsea as she handed them each a small rectangular box wrapped in metallic pink paper and tied with a matching ribbon. Chelsea had insisted on going last, and Emily had a feeling it was because her gifts would be the most impressive — or at least the most expensive. "I didn't know we were supposed to."

"Well, it wasn't exactly a rule," said Morgan. "But it was suggested. We didn't want anyone to feel pressured to go out and buy things."

"Especially after we all worked so hard to pay our way for the ski trip," Carlie pointed out as they opened Chelsea's packages. Beneath the shiny pink paper was a long, narrow, black velvet box with a fancy gold B in one corner.

"Ooh," said Amy with excitement, "This looks like it's from Bernstein's. My dad gave my mom a diamond necklace that was in a box like this."

"Well, don't worry," said Chelsea. "No diamonds are involved."

The girls all laughed, but no one had opened a box yet.

"Come on," Chelsea said eagerly. "Go ahead and see what's inside."

Emily ran her finger over the plush velvet box. She knew that Bernstein's was the jewelry store downtown. She'd never been in the shop, but she could tell by the window displays that it was a pretty nice store — and expensive. The other girls were beginning to ooh and aw, so Emily knew she needed to open her box too. And when she did, she saw that it contained what looked like a nice charm bracelet.

"See the little school bus," gushed Chelsea. "Isn't it just too cute?"

"It's like our bus," said Carlie.

"These are beautiful," said Amy as she held her bracelet up to the light. "They must've been expensive."

"Not as much as gold ones would've been," said Chelsea. "Mom nixed that idea right off the bat. But these are sterling silver." She held out her own wrist now. "See, I have a bracelet too. Obviously, the school bus represents our clubhouse, and the initial is for your first name, so we don't get them mixed up."

"What about you and me?" said Carlie. "We're both C's."

"Yeah, I figured that could be a problem, so I got an L put on mine, for my last name. And see the little snowboard. That's for our upcoming ski trip."

"Cool," said Amy.

"Yeah, thanks," said Morgan. "These are really nice."

They all thanked her, and everyone seemed happy. And yet Emily was curious. She wondered if Chelsea's bracelets were meant to replace their old beaded ones that she and Morgan had made last summer. Still, she decided not to bring this up. She didn't want to seem ungrateful or to stir up any problems at their Christmas party. Besides, what was the harm in wearing two bracelets? Because Emily knew that she had no intention of giving up her old one. It meant too much to her.

Next they had refreshments. And as they munched, they joked and chatted and enjoyed their own little party of five. In the background, cheerful Christmas music played, and for a moment, Emily just sat there looking at her four good friends. She still couldn't believe how close she had come to losing all this. As a result, she thought of her dad, but these were not happy thoughts. In fact, every time he came to mind, her stomach would tie itself into a tight knot, and she would begin to feel a combination of anger and fear. More and more, she felt that she hated him. And sometimes she wished he were dead.

"What's wrong, Em?" asked Morgan.

"Yeah," said Carlie. "You look kinda bummed. Is everything okay?"

"Sorry." Emily shrugged. "I guess I was just remembering stuff ... you know ... about how my family almost left

Boscoe Bay for good and everything."

"Well, don't think about that," said Amy. "You're here. You're with us. And everything is cool."

"That's right," said Chelsea. "Celebrate!"

And so Emily pasted a big smile on her face and pretended to be totally happy. But underneath it all, she was not. Underneath it all, she was just plain mad — she was angry at her dad and for how his presence in her town and in her life was nothing but a great big pain. And it felt like her anger was starting to eat away at her.

chapter thirteen

Emily could hardly believe that it was the day before
Christmas. So much had happened this past week, it had
felt as if the time had flown by. And now it was December 24th, and Emily planned to spend a quiet day at home.
Mom and Kyle both had to work during the day, and
Morgan was next door helping her mom and grandma get
things together for their Christmas. She had invited Emily
to join them, but since Emily had been practically living
over there the past few days, she decided to give them a
break today. Plus, her family would be going over to celebrate Christmas with them tomorrow anyway.

For today, Emily's plan was to wrap Kyle's and Mom's
Christmas presents and then straighten up the house.
But she'd finished that a lot quicker than she'd expected.
Her presents were already tucked beneath their tree, and
their house was all tidy and neat. She walked around a bit,
just taking a moment to enjoy the results of her efforts.
Their place was really pretty cozy now. So much better
than when they'd first come here last spring. In fact, that
seemed like a long time ago now.

She remembered how lost she'd felt when they moved into this house. It was so much smaller and shabbier than the house they'd left behind. But even so, Emily had been relieved to get away from her angry father. It had been worth the sacrifice. Now — if only he hadn't tracked them down — life might be nearly perfect. She'd been trying not to dwell on the fact that her dad was still in town. It was too disturbing. But at least, according to their lawyer anyway, he was still in jail. Although the rumor was that he was trying to borrow bail money from his family in Idaho. Probably from Aunt Becky. She was still pretty clueless when it came to the true character of her "baby brother." She had always tried to protect him, always acted as if he was blameless.

Despite her resolve not to, Emily thought about her dad. She sat down beneath the Christmas tree and wondered what it felt like to be locked up in jail. What would if be like to be restricted to a small space like that? She remembered the book she'd just read, and how Anne Frank and her family lived in an attic space for several years. In a way, that must've felt like prison too. And yet they had done nothing wrong.

Then Emily wondered how it would feel to be in jail during Christmas. How would it feel to think about other families enjoying each other, enjoying all the fun parts of Christmas? She felt an unexpected jab of pity just then — sort of how she felt when she thought about Derrick Smith being stuck in juvenile detention. Not that both those bullies didn't deserve to be locked up. They did. But the image of her dad sitting alone behind bars made her feel sad. Okay, it was sad mixed with mad. And she definitely didn't want him to get out. In fact, it worried her a lot to think that someone like Aunt Becky might possibly post his bail.

If only things could be different — if only her dad could be different — but that didn't seem possible. As it was, she hoped he'd be stuck in jail for a long, long time. She hoped he'd never get out. When she considered how much he'd hurt her family ... how he'd frightened and threatened her very best friend. Well, Emily really didn't feel too sorry for that man. Not really.

Still, she knew enough about the Bible and Jesus' teachings by now to know that Christians were supposed to follow Jesus' example and to forgive those who hurt them. She also knew they were supposed to pray for people who were enemies or wanted to hurt them. The truth was she had never really done it much before. She'd never really had the need to do it. Until now. And yet she wondered how she could forgive a man who had brought so much pain into her life? How was that even possible?

Emily stretched out on the matted-down carpet beneath their Christmas tree. She put her hands behind her head and closed her eyes as she pondered these troubling questions.

It felt wrong to *not* forgive ... and yet how was it possible to forgive someone you still felt mad at, someone who had hurt you badly, and someone you sometimes hated? She went round and round with these questions until she finally knew it was useless — there really was no good answer. Just more questions.

That's when she did what her pastor often recommended. She took the whole thing to God. She asked him to show her what she needed to do about this perplexing problem. She asked God to guide her. And, just like that, the answer came to her. And it seemed simple enough. But simple didn't always come easily.

First of all, she knew she needed to forgive her dad, and second of all, she knew she needed to pray for him. The problem was she didn't know how to do that. It seemed impossible. So, right then and there, she asked God to help her. And, right then and there, although she didn't really feel like it, she decided it was time to forgive her dad.

So she told God she could only do this thing with his help, and she asked him to help her. Then help seemed to come, and she actually did forgive her dad. She even said the words out loud. More than that, she actually prayed for her dad. She asked God to reach out to him, to help him see what he was doing wrong. "And help him," she prayed, "to see that he needs you, dear God. Show my dad that he can't change and live a good life without your help. And tell him that you love him. Thank you. Amen."

When Emily opened her eyes and looked up at the Christmas tree, she realized the colored lights were all blurry and fuzzy now … because she was crying. And that's when she knew that it was for real. She knew that God really had helped her to make this step to forgive her dad. She also realized that it felt as if a heavy weight had been lifted from her — and that for the first time in a long time she felt truly happy.

She felt so happy that she even put on some music — a lively Christmas CD that Morgan had given to her just yesterday. And Emily cranked it up and did a little happy dance around the Christmas tree. And as she danced, she thanked God for helping her. And she thanked him for sending his only Son to share forgiveness with every-one — even her dad!

Then when she was too tired to keep dancing, she col-lapsed onto a chair. And that's when she got the strongest urge to write her dad a letter. She still had some Christmas cards leftover from the ones she'd given to her friends and few special teachers at school. She took one out and wrote his name on the inside of the card. Then she took out a clean piece of paper and wrote a heartfelt note to her dad.

Dear Dad,

You're probably surprised to get this card from me, but I was thinking about you today. And because I'm a

Christian now, I know that God wants me to forgive you for all the times you hurt Mom and Kyle and me. So I just prayed a little while ago, and God helped me to forgive you. I'm also going to be praying for you now because the Bible says to pray for your enemies. I don't like to think that my dad is my enemy, but you've done some pretty mean things to us ... the kinds of things that enemies do to people they don't like. So, anyway, I will be praying for you.

I don't know how long you'll be in jail, and for your sake, I hope it's not too long. But I hope it's long enough for you to think about all the things you've done and the way you've hurt us. I hope you stay there long enough to feel sorry for your mistakes. And then I hope you'll go back to Idaho and leave us alone. I heard enough of what Mom's lawyer said to know that the law is on our side now. We've been in Oregon for more than six months, so that means you can't force us to leave. You probably know this too. Anyway, I hope that someday Kyle and I will be able to talk to you. Someday when you don't want to hurt us anymore. And I hope that your life gets better, Dad. I hope that you get some help with your anger problem. And I hope that this Christmas, even though it's probably hard, is like a turning point for you. I'm praying that you will ask God for help and that you'll give your heart to him. I know he's helped me through some pretty tough times.

From Emily

Emily looked at the ending of her note. *From Emily* sounded a little formal and sort of mean. So she crossed out "From" and replaced it with "Love." She figured that would make God happy since Christians were supposed to love others, whether others deserved it or not. Then she put the note inside the Christmas card, wrote Dad's name on the front, put on her coat, and walked to town. It was actually a pretty nice day. No rain, no wind. Of course, there was no snow either. That was probably the only thing she missed from her old home in Idaho. But she would rather be here without snow than in Idaho with three feet of it. Besides, she would have plenty of snow in a couple of days.

It was fun walking through town. Christmas music was being played outside, and the town's Christmas tree was lit up, as well as colorful lights in most of the shops. People were busily hurrying around, probably doing their last-minute tasks before Christmas. Emily smiled at people and said hello to ones she knew. She even paused and put some change into the Salvation Army pot. Then she walked on to City Hall. She wasn't absolutely certain that her dad was in the jail there, but she figured there was a good chance that he was.

Then, as soon as she went through the entrance, she felt self-conscious. She wondered if she was making a big mistake in coming here. And what if Mom got mad at her for doing this? Still, Emily knew in her heart that it was the right thing to do. And so she went up to the front desk.

"Can I help you?" asked a policewoman.

"Uh, I have something to be delivered," said Emily. She set the envelope on the desk. "It's for my dad."

The woman smiled. "Oh, is he a policeman?"

"Uh, no …" Emily took in a quick breath. "I think he's in jail here."

The woman nodded. "Oh …"

"Do you think someone could give him this Christmas card for me?"

"It will have to be opened and inspected first," the woman told her. "Are you okay with that?"

Emily shrugged. "Yeah, I guess so."

"It's not that we don't trust you. It's just a policy. Some people try to sneak things in here — things that aren't allowed."

"Oh, well, there's nothing like that in there."

The policewoman smiled. "No, I didn't think so. And I'm sure your dad will appreciate that you thought of him."

"I thought he might be feeling a little sad, you know, being in here for Christmas. I mean I think he *needs* to be here and everything. Still, it's probably hard on him."

"Well, if it makes you feel any better, I've heard that the Christmas dinner served here is pretty tasty."

Emily smiled. "That's good."

"You have a Merry Christmas now."

"You too." Then Emily turned and walked out. Sure, it hadn't been the easiest thing in the world to do, but she was so glad she'd done it. And she knew she had only been able to do it with God's help. She also knew this was going to be a really great Christmas.

Talk It Up!

Want free books?
First looks at the best new fiction?
Awesome exclusive merchandise?

We want to hear from you!

Give us your opinions on titles, covers, and stories.
Join the Z Street Team.

Email us at zstreetteam@zondervan.com
to sign up today!

Also—Friend us on Facebook!

www.facebook.com/goodteenreads

- Video Trailers
- Connect with your favorite authors
- Sneak peeks at new releases
- Giveaways
- Fun discussions
- And much more!

.com